She's Nobody . . .
but Everybody

by

Nancy Desrosiers

uBT
PRESS

This is a work of fiction. Names, characters, places, and incidents are either the product of the author's imagination or are used fictitiously. Any resemblance to actual persons, living or dead, business establishments, events, or locales is entirely coincidental.

ISBN 0-9721489-3-0

Published by
UNIFIED BUSINESS TECHNOLOGIES PRESS
AMHERST, NEW HAMPSHIRE 03031
www.unifiedbiztech.com

October 2003

10 9 8 7 6 5 4 3 2

Edited by

Peter G. Markwith

To
Amanda
My Granddaughter

Acknowledgments

I reserve this page exclusively for the purpose of extending my sincerest thanks to Mother Thecla Merlo, my husband Chick, my niece Marea, Jan Spry, Julie Davidson, Cindy Cloutier and Pat Coughlin for their invaluable knowledge, suggestions, editorial assistance, computer expertise, time and, most valued of all, confidence.

Prologue

Although our present society constantly shifts its values and has now chosen to abandon courtesy, benevolence and compassion, these qualities linger in a nursing home high in the White Mountains of New Hampshire where autumn waves goodbye as winter slowly approaches.

On this particular fading afternoon in the year 2025, graceful, undulating pines and maples validate the wind as they sway like ballerinas in lush green tutus. An elderly lady enjoys the performance from her rocking chair.

Her thoughts wander down the lonely lane of yesteryear.

Leaves, lovely leaves, you've been swaying in the wind for centuries.

I wonder why time always comes to mind? Only natural I suppose. Our lives are so governed by it. Yet, no matter what happens to us, nothing is catastrophic enough to stop time; it just keeps moving on and will as long as the world exists. How foolish to think we've set limits on it with our seconds, hours, days, months and years. Good heavens, they mean nothing to ageless, unstoppable time. It bows to no bounds.

No matter, I've been doing my best to defy it for as long as I can remember. Even so, somehow I've reached the age of ninety-five—just couldn't hold back time, no matter how hard I pulled on its selfish, old tail.

That mighty mountain over there is thinking, "She's only a babe." Well, these rickety, old bones strongly refute that observation.

Do you suppose it's possible there's something else the good Lord wants me to do?

I've always had a million questions for Him. Even back when I was sixteen I wondered who I was and why I was here. I remember inquiring one afternoon as I gazed up at the sky He'd painted His favorite shade of blue. He never answered but left it up to me to find out for myself. And I did.

Well, if there is a task He wants done, He'd better let me know about it pretty soon because, thanks to the intuition He gives his ancient and faithful friends, I'm pretty sure I'm not going to be enjoying the pleasure of this rocker much longer.

I'm ready though. I don't think I'd care to be young today. From what I read in the newspapers the world has gone completely haywire. Imagine, developers seriously considering moving business to the moon. Well, no matter, the moon will always be the most romantic light in the world.

But I don't suppose there's much romance floating around these days. My heart is sad for the young and adolescent. Their lives seem so bogged down with indulgent self-gratification. Good heavens, there's no happiness to be found in self; it's much too heavy a burden. I wish I could lighten up those lives a little, add a little romance and a few flights of fancy.

I'd love to introduce the kids to radio back in the days when it sparked imaginations and turned evenings into havens of make-believe. I know they'd love Charlie McCarthy as much as I loved that capricious, wooden doll. Funny how he never seemed a doll. Edgar Bergen made him so real. I fancied Charlie with red, curly hair peeking out from under a brown tweed cap. Anne pictured Charlie with…Anne, my dear, dear friend. It's been so long since you left the world behind. But you didn't really leave, did you? Oh, I know you come to visit now and then.

Remember how you insisted Charlie had straight, black hair sitting under a bright green and yellow plaid beanie. Well, we settled that little dispute didn't we? It was your suggestion to send for the life-size, cardboard likeness offered by the radio station. Weren't we surprised when he arrived with a monocle perched on his right eye twinkling from under the brim of a black top hat?

Oh my, haven't heard of anything like Charlie in a long, long time. I suppose the art of ventriloquism has gone the way of most things that gave our lives back then a respite from the sacrifices we endured without question—sacrifices certainly more preferable than the onus of self everyone carries around today.

I'm so thankful just for the sheer fun and buoyancy that love, sacrifice and helping others have brought to my life all these years.

The old lady smiles nostalgically as she quietly enjoys the scenic view that inspires so many reflective journeys; content to be here far away from the world she relinquished so long ago.

As she watches, the sun slowly sinks behind her high and mighty mountain. When the orange hue is but a wink, she sighs and rises from her chair ignoring the pain she's lived with now for so long. She slowly saunters into the house she now calls home, as do many of her contemporaries—most of whom are younger, but one or two are older.

The stately, white "home" can be seen for miles around peeking through a myriad of trees. Its deep green shutters stand at attention against the stark white clapboards as if guarding each gleaming window. A wide porch skirted by a white spindled railing encircles the house in the same way a ring surrounds the moon on the eve of a storm. The color of its many rocking chairs mimics that of the shutters. The chairs stand motionless along the entire length—some side by side, others secluded with white wicker tables.

Tourists roaming far below look up in admiration at this jewel sparkling through pines and maples high above the Wentworth Golf Course in Jackson, a quaint, little town on the other side of an ancient covered bridge.

She's Nobody ... but Everybody

Emma's time on earth may well be coming to an end but she doesn't consider that fact a good enough reason to sit back and ignore another's need.

She is ninety-five years old but alert and ready to face the challenges of each new day—at least most days.

Perhaps not a lady in the grand sense of the word, she is definitely a lady in the truer sense—gracious, dependable, caring and witty. Emma is a portrait of graceful aging—tall and thin, ever impeccably dressed with pure white hair pulled back in a French twist that complements her oval face and enhances sparkling, speckled-green eyes.

A private person, she finds her own company quite satisfactory. Unfortunately, she has often been misunderstood and thought unpropitious. But this aspect of her personality serves Emma well now that she has long since survived family and friends.

Loneliness is never allowed to creep into her solitude, for it is one of the many things Emma has always considered a waste of time. However, she does appreciate it when the spirits of her loved ones come to visit now and then here in this stately white house with green shutters—her remote and quiescent "home" standing in the center of surroundings she's known and loved all her life.

The occasional, spectral tarriances are why she makes sure to look her best at all times.

When weather permits, Emma enjoys spending time on the front porch. She can remember her grandmother calling it the piazza. Her chair sits alone to the far right facing a panoramic view of Mount Washington, the highest peak in the White Mountains of New Hampshire. She'll rock contentedly for hours, lulled by the sound of the floorboards.

"Squeak. Squeak. Squeak."

She doesn't find the sound annoying, more rhythmical—soothing really.

No one but Emma sits in *that* chair, nor is another chair ever placed beside it—not because she's unfriendly, quite the contrary, it's just that others are immersed in memories of their own. At times, tiring of her own past, she wishes the house could share with her the secrets it gleans listening to those who dwell within—the elderly do have a tendency to think out loud.

What a revealing book this *lady* could write.

As we peek in on Emma, a gloriously colorful, fall morning has inspired her to slip on a white turtleneck sweater over a brown tweed skirt that doesn't quite reach her ankles. She puts on the shoes she refers to as "my loafers," and the creamy pearls she places around her long, slender neck extend to her waistline. They were a gift from her husband on their fifteenth wedding anniversary.

As she leaves the room she reaches for the warm tweed jacket hanging on her tall mahogany coat rack and walks down the hall toward the elevator.

After breakfast Emma begins her daily stroll around the porch. When she reaches the rear of the house, she stops to peer at the top of a head covered with thick, black, curly hair being blown haphazardly by the passing breeze. It is all that can be seen above the back of a presidential rocker where the young man sits every morning—alone and silent.

For some reason, on this particular morning she stops and wonders why he sits at the back of the house where there is no view. But what's more puzzling is why he's living here at all. Why would he want to live in a house where the inhabitants are all waiting their turn to greet St. Peter? As she stares at the black hair wafting above the woven reed of his chair, a compelling sense of sorrow draws her toward him. She takes two or three steps before some inner perception warns her he shouldn't be disturbed.

Hesitating but a second, Emma continues slowly along the porch deep in thought. By the time she reaches her rocking chair she has decided to ask Catherine, one of the more pleasant of the nurses, about the young fellow with the black curly hair. She rocks back and forth, back and forth, and waits.

Catherine appears at the doorway.

"Ah, Catherine there you are. Do you have a minute to talk?"

Catherine hops up onto the railing and adjusts her white uniform—crisp as a cracker. Her cropped, curly, red hair shines brightly above Irish green eyes.

"Catherine, please tell me about the young man with the curly black hair who sits at the back of the house."

The Irish green eyes sadden.

"Sure and his name's Luke Turnbridge and he's twenty years old. His motorcycle went out from under him about a year and a half ago. Sure and he lay in a coma for about a year.

But last November he opened his eyes. Poor lad he couldn't see—blinded for life he was. Couldn't remember a thing either and hasn't remembered a thing since. He's lucky though in one way, his parents are rich and can do for him."

Emma shakes her head in response to the sadness creeping into her heart as she listens.

"He's not responded to therapy. Everybody's agreed nothin's goin' to help him if he doesn't help himself. For now, they've sent him up here hopin', I guess, if he's left alone, he'll find his own way back. His Mum told me she agreed only 'cause she's desperate and she's countin' on Luke gatherin' strength from the mountains. She hopes they'll help the lad return from wherever it is he's gone."

Catherine's brogue, which to Emma's delight Catherine hasn't managed to lose completely, can't seem to lighten this hapless conversation.

"Sure and the poor woman feels it's worth a try for a little bit."

"Why is he always sitting out back?" Emma inquires, pointing to the rear of the house.

"I put him there. Luke doesn't care. It just seemed to me I ought to be usin' the chairs out front for my people who can see the view."

"I suppose you're right. Can the boy hear?"

"I guess so. Nobody's ever said he couldn't. Sure and he can, 'cause sometimes it seems to me he's listenin' for somethin'."

Emma looks off into the distance and Catherine hops off the railing. As she starts to walk away, Emma calls out to her.

"How is Sean handling his freshman year?"

Catherine turns. Her face shines like the sun for she is so proud of her Sean for having received a full football scholarship from Dartmouth College.

Emma raises an arm as if shielding her eyes from its glow.

"I don't need an answer. Your countenance tells all."

Laughing, Catherine pulls a new picture out of her pocket and hands it to Emma, whose smile reflects her love for all youth.

"Has he given any thought to a major?"

"Sure and he's gonna be an architect like his Da always wanted to be."

Emma's smile broadens.

"I'm glad Catherine. It's a satisfying profession if one has the aptitude."

"Sure and that may be so, but I'm a bit apprehensive. He's not like his Da or his older brother Pat. Sean's a free spirit. He doesn't wanna be an architect. Sure and he just thinks he should be."

"Oh, why do you say that?"

" 'Cause Pat joined the Navy."

"He what? When, and for goodness sake why?"

"Left two weeks ago. Long as I can remember Pat's talked about the ocean. When the lads were little their Da and I'd take 'em to the beach for picnics. I never realized what that great big ocean was doin' to my Pat. The mornin' he left he looked down at me from that six-foot frame of his and told me the mountains had always smothered him. Emma, I cried for hours after he left. You know better'n most around here how much I love these grand peaks, the notches and rocky ledges. Why I could stand and watch those splashin' streams soak the tough flumes for hours. Imagine, the lad's been stifled by them for all these years.

"Sure and that's why Sean feels at least one son should fulfill their Da's dream. But he's an artist, Emma. He loves to paint the peace and the roarin' rage of those trees and streams out there. How in the name of heaven can one son feel smothered by what the other uses to free up his inner feelin's? Sure and I can't even imagine my Sean sittin' all day in front of a drawin' board. His talent should be takin' him down another road. Oh, but he loved his Da so.

"Sure and I shouldn't be botherin' you with all this Emma."

"Now don't be silly Catherine. If there's one thing I'm good at it's listening. And I've certainly got plenty of time."

"Thanks Emma."

She glances at her watch.

"Sure and I could be sittin' here all day talkin' to you but I'd better hop to."

As she disappears through the doorway she calls over her shoulder, "Sure and we'll be talkin' again soon."

Emma's "Indeed we shall." softly accompanies an unnoticed wave of her hand.

"Indeed we shall."

The following morning, as Catherine helps serve breakfast, Emma waylays her again and asks if she will put Luke's chair out front beside her own. Catherine doesn't hide her surprise but assures Emma she'll be glad to move Luke's chair, then adds, "Luke doesn't care where he sits."

Early that afternoon as Emma walks out onto the porch, a wide smile spreads across her face. She stops for a moment to think about what she'll say to this young man sitting quiet and still. Then walks slowly toward him and settles comfortably in her chair. She rocks and listens.

"Squeak. Squeak, Squeak."

Her mind wanders off into the soothing sound. For how long she's not sure.

"Good afternoon young man. I guess I dozed off for a minute. Isn't the air refreshing?"

No response.

She continues.

"Catherine tells me you're called Luke. My name is Emma, and I'm going to share a secret with you. I am ninety-five years old. Ladies don't usually admit their age, but I feel being honest with one another is very important. Don't you?"

Silence.

Undaunted, she goes on.

"I sit here many a day, if the weather behaves, and think about the world back in the twentieth century when I was as young as you are. I love to look back and think about all the amazing things I did."

Emma takes a moment to contemplate the silent young man.

"But I guess, on the whole, I was pretty ordinary, whatever that means. Oh, there were probably a few things I shouldn't have done, but I have few regrets. The one thing I do regret though is never having been a storyteller. You know, a person who sits on a high stool in the middle of a group of youngsters, or adults, and tells stories. A storyteller came to our library one day when I was a little girl. We all gathered around her, and she asked if one of us would give her a subject. I did, and she told the most wonderful story about an elephant. I've always wanted to do that. Take some simple, ordinary thing or situation and make it shine."

"Squeak. Squeak. Squeak."

Emma rocks and listens to the soothing sound before trying again.

"I guess I don't have to tell you young man, this world belongs to you. It's yours to enjoy, explore and improve. We elders prefer to relive the past we spent a lifetime creating purposely for our old age."

Emma turns her head toward Luke. A chill runs down her spine as she looks into the cold, blue marbles inert in his face of stone.

Later, up in her room Emma sits by the window watching evening begin its journey toward night. Her heart cries for a young man with cold, glassy eyes.

Far better than most, she is able to understand his devastation. Her loss had been even more devouring.

She wants to help him. But how? Tears trickle down her cheeks and she fumbles for the handkerchief in her pocket, then hesitates. Should she wipe away the dampness or let her awakened grief have its way? She allows the tears to flow freely and ponders the advisability of stepping back into the heartache.

But, creeping through her sorrow, a thought catches her attention and she says aloud, "Of course, there's no other way. I must paint for this young man a verbal picture of a life's journey—its joys, its woes and the importance of accepting whatever comes along. No one else seems to have the kind of time it will take to do that. Oh, but I have all the time in the world.

And then Emma, totally out of character, lets go of her fortitude and slips back to the horrible, fateful day that changed forever the course she had chosen for her life.

It was a Saturday in springtime. The birds were having a field day, crocuses pushed through the enlivened soil and ski conditions in Tuckerman Ravine were perfect.

High in the White Mountains, "Tuck," pitched at a fifty-five degree angle, indomitable and covered with fifty-to-seventy feet of snow awaited the hordes that would challenge its bowl—the only spot left in New England where skiers could race the boards even into July and sometimes August.

These hardy souls never complained about the lack of tows, for they looked forward to the climb, skis strapped to their backs. They couldn't wait to absorb the surrounding, indescribable beauty only they would see—their reward for answering "Tuck's" challenge. Not all skiers were willing to defy its steep, precipitous walls and weather conditions that so often changed in an instant, turning the ravine into a devastating killer unmercifully hurtling down tremendous sections of ice and snow, weighing tons.

At five o'clock that morning, Emma and her husband Matt, a history professor at the University of New Hampshire, climbed into the front seat of their Ford station wagon. Monique, their only child and a member of the UNH graduating class the year before, climbed into the back seat. Matt drove north up into the White Mountains heading toward Route 16 and Pinkham Notch. Emma, a skier but not a climber, had come along to share as much of the day as she could with those she loved more than anyone else in the world.

They stopped in North Conway for a cup of coffee and took the opportunity to stretch their legs before traveling the last half hour it would take to reach the Appalachian Mountain Club hut, where they would begin their climb up to Tuckerman Ravine.

Upon reaching the hut, they unloaded their gear, locked the car and hiked up the Fire Trail as far as the Tuckerman Shelter, affectionately referred to as Howard Johnson's by those who counted on its amenities. It was bustling with anxious skiers and hikers. Emma, Matt and Monique found a table and sat down to enjoy a cup of hot coffee and a doughnut.

After discussing how long Matt and Monique would probably be gone and where they would all stop for dinner on the way home, Matt and Monique decided they'd better get started for the ravine. Gulping down the last mouthful of coffee, they ran out onto the porch to gather up their equipment. They both deposited a kiss on Emma's cheek and ran down the steps. But turned to wave one more goodbye. She waved back and promised to watch from the porch of the shelter.

Emma stood by the railing until they disappeared into the woods. She turned then, eyeing a rather lonesome looking rocking chair sitting quietly just a few feet away. She decided it was as good a place as any to wait for Matt and Monique to climb above the tree line.

As Monique and her father hiked along a trail near Hermit Lake she told him about plans she was making with her friend Emily to spend at least a year touring the country. Matt, of course, had his concerns and was about to mention a few when Monique, not paying attention to where she was going, fell over a loose rock and tumbled down a small incline. She sat up in the middle of a pile of dried leaves and twigs laughing as she watched Matt rush down toward her. He started to laugh too when he saw she was all right. They were both thinking the same thing—now that's something Emma would have done. When they climbed back up onto the trail and continued on their way, they shared the warmth that always followed when they discussed Emma and her little idiosyncrasies. They were so wrapped up in this time together they almost missed their destination.

Meanwhile, Emma, her binoculars at the ready around her neck, had gotten herself a cup of coffee and now sat watching for two red sweaters and a large red flag that would be flying in the wind from the top of Matt's skis.

As she waited she noticed a young man sitting on the porch railing. She was curious about why he wasn't climbing the bowl and got up to inquire. It was immediately obvious to her that he could not see the outstanding view presenting itself before him. They talked for awhile and, though she didn't ask, he told her he'd been blinded three years before when he'd lost control of his skis and hit a tree. She did ask why he came. He smiled and told her he loved to come to the ravine in the spring to feel the air and see in his mind what so many never see with their eyes. She smiled for she knew that the courage that had brought him to Tuckerman Ravine in the first place brought him back each year in the spring.

The air was not cold but definitely nippy. The red wool sweaters Emma had knit for Matt and Monique felt warm and comfortable for the sun that Saturday had decided to shine somewhere else. As they climbed they laughed and laughed, seemingly at nothing or maybe at just being alive.

Emma went back to her rocking chair and looked through the binoculars. There they were—her two red dots against the white snow. How happy she was to see them. She watched their progress while at the same time observing other skiers climbing all the way to the headwall. Matt and Monique were climbing only half way. She loved watching them all—those shushing down the wall of the bowl and others who seemed to be gracefully dancing their way down—the whole spectacle a ballet intermingled with an Olympic, down-hill race.

Emma adjusted the binoculars—she always had a difficult time keeping them focused—and could see that Matt and Monique had a ways to go before they started down. She watched for a few more minutes then got up to go into the restaurant for an English muffin and another cup of coffee. As she sat at the counter, an explosive, devastating crack-like sound filled the air. The shelter shook. Had the earth split in two? That's how it sounded. Emma ran out the door and leaned on the railing scanning the ravine.

"What's happened?"

A huge segment of ice had broken off the top of the headwall into the bowl and was spiraling downward. Emma grabbed the binoculars and scanned the area where she had last seen Matt and Monique. She could see nothing but moving, hurtling ice. She stood mesmerized until an arm gently squeezing her shoulders brought her back to reality. She looked up at the young man and then focused her binoculars again on the ravine. She saw them—two red dots trying to run through the soft, deep snow. She screamed when she saw the ice and snow careen toward the two most important people in her world. If only they'd had on their skis they might have had a chance. She knew they weren't going to make it.

Skis wouldn't have been much help. No one could be seen in the bowl.

Why couldn't she move? She needed to move if she was going to help, but what could she do? Then she spotted the Ski Patrol rushing up to where she'd last seen Matt and Monique.

She grabbed the binoculars. Would they be in time? She knew no one could survive if they remained buried more than twenty minutes. Could they find them all? Emma watched the frantic digging in horror until toboggans, waiting on the snow, sent a shiver of eeriness through her soul. Would they be vehicles of rescue or biers?

The young man never let go of her. She absorbed his strength when the two red dots were lifted from the snow and placed on the toboggans. Emma fainted when blankets were placed full length over both biers.

Dabbing at the tears running down her cheeks, Emma straightens her back.

"Come on now, that's enough of that. You'll be seeing them both soon, but right now you've got a job to do. Where do you think would be the best place to start?"

A waterfall cascades from the sky for the next three days and gives Emma the time she needs to pull her plan together.

Several years before, the daughter of a former resident donated an extensive library to the home. It's here we find Emma busy looking for a poem which periodically runs through her mind. She needs the poem now but can't remember its name or who wrote it. Sure of the poet's ethnic background she's been researching every German bard she can find.

When day four arrives with sunbeams dancing on Emma's nose, she smiles as she slips out from under the covers and rests her feet on the small Oriental rug on the floor by her bed. Each morning this little ritual allows her to organize her thoughts before attempting to meet the challenge of a new day.

She gets up and goes through her morning routine before putting on her snappy red suit. She feels a necessity for red this morning.

Walking into the dining room with a jaunty step, she greets everyone with a wide grin and a cheery, "Good Morning!" A few greetings are mumbled in return.

Emma shrugs her shoulders and chooses a seat by the window. When her breakfast is served, she tries not to swallow the toast and oatmeal too fast, but she wants to get out onto the porch.

"Marie," she calls to the sweet, young girl who serves the meals and helps out in a hundred other ways, "I'm going out on the porch. Would you mind bringing me a fresh cup of coffee?"

"I'd be glad to Mrs. Duprey."

Emma has enjoyed but a few sips of the fresh coffee when Catherine arrives with Luke. She sits him down in the chair beside Emma. All is quiet except for the familiar song being sung by the floorboards under Emma's chair.

As nonchalantly as she can, Emma begins the poem Goethe wrote many years before:

"We must not hope to be mowers
And to gather the ripe gold ears,
Unless we have first been sowers
And watered the furrows with tears.
It is not just as we take it,
This mystical world of ours.
Life's field will yield as we make it,
A harvest of thorns or of flowers."

"I read that poem a long time ago and have never forgotten it—especially those last two lines. 'Life's field will yield as we make it, A harvest of thorns or of flowers.'

"What are Life's thorns and what her flowers? Not easy questions to answer when one ponders the fact that thorns protect each velvet rose. Food for thought though. Maybe I'll just think about it for awhile."

Luke stares into his black world, greatly annoyed with the constancy of the intruding voice.

Oh shut up, lady.

Emma rocks to the rhythm of the floorboards till Marie announces lunch.

Sitting alone in the sunny dining room, she enjoys a bowl of hot chicken soup and a steaming cup of tea. As she takes her last sip of tea, Emma suspects that perhaps she has said enough for today. Instead of going out onto the porch for the afternoon she walks toward the elevator. Stepping out onto the second floor she decides to spend a few quiet moments in the tiny chapel before going to her room where the adventures of *The Count of Monte Cristo* wait for her on a table by the large, overstuffed chair she's recently had recovered in a lively, bright yellow print.

Catherine had advised against having her chair placed by the drafty window, but Emma couldn't imagine it being anywhere else.

The following morning, an aura of anticipation surrounds Emma as she presses the prettiest comb in her drawer into the fold of her French twist, smiling at the mirror's approval. She turns and carefully smoothes the pleated skirt of her lavender silk dress. She had bought the dress because of its becoming Irish-lace collar. When she was a young girl, her grandmother advised her never to purchase a dress unless the collar complimented her coloring and the shape of her face.

"I must look extra special," she says out loud.

Special, for today Emma hopes Luke's long journey back to the world of realty will begin. She looks into the mirror and asks its reflection, "Will he listen to my stories or will the wind carry my words up, over and beyond the top of my mighty mountain?"

Going to the window, she stares out at the sweeping view which slowly fades into a fear that her plan for Luke will not be enough to help him overcome the desolation she knows must engulf him.

What would it be like not having anything to think about? Suddenly, the swishing of leaves back and forth shifts to a howling wind that reclaims Emma from her anxiety, and she becomes absorbed in the astonishing spectacle performing outside the window.

What would I do if I couldn't watch the wonders going on around me?

She tries desperately to imagine being adrift in a dark, unfathomable abyss, but her endeavor fails.

She crosses the room to get a sweater out of the drawer. On her way downstairs in the elevator, Emma banishes her fears and vows to grab Luke away from Luke.

During breakfast, she reviews her plan to verbally illustrate the importance of sharing one's talents and gifts with a world beyond self.

First I must make him understand how unimportant it is when life starts to record itself. How well I know twenty is only the beginning.

Emma sighs and sips her coffee as she contemplates the probability of her accomplishing this monumental task with only the modest stories of a young girl's efforts to bring meaning into her own life.

But they're all I have. I've always been a nobody—just like everybody. I can only pray my stories will trigger in this lost, young man a desire to allow his life its opportunities so he can build a past to call upon when he's left behind by a hurtling, indifferent world.

Her memories and his hearing are the only tools Emma has; she hopes there are more. Is it only the events of his life that are gone or has everything vanished? Does he know he's sitting in a chair? Does he know the color red? Does he remember words? Could that be why he hasn't responded to anyone?

Emma prays fervently that Luke will at least be able to understand what she is saying. She also prays that if he could once paint, write poetry, compose music or make people laugh, he still can, and eventually will.

She emerges from the dining room followed by Marie carrying a tray with two cups of fresh coffee. The wind has died down to a murmur. Even so, Emma feels a chill.

"Marie, would you mind getting my shawl? I left it up on my yellow chair by the window. Thank you, you're a dear."

Placing her tray carefully on the white wicker table, Marie smiles and nods.

"I'll be right back."

Emma looks over at Luke and hopes he will hear her smile.

"Good morning young man. Would you like a fresh cup of coffee?"

"Churlee. Churlee. Churlee."

Only the rich and varied song of a purple finch fills the air.

Marie returns with Emma's shawl and hurries off down the porch.

The light, carefree wind ruffles Emma's white hair as she drinks her steaming-hot coffee. Along with the heat of the sun, it warms her ancient and fragile bones. As the purple finch warbles and the wind transforms trees into ballerinas, she begins.

"Do you mind being my guinea pig Luke? I'd like to try my hand at storytelling. Let's start with the simple fact of being born.

"My mother's window—I called it Mama's window because she liked to sit by it late in the afternoon—did not have an ocean view or that of a majestic mountain. It didn't look out from a palatial palace, magnificent mansion or even an ordinary family home. It did gleam brightly in the wall of her bedroom on the second floor of an apartment building hidden away on a quiet street in Collier, New Hampshire. I've often wondered what was outside that window that captured her attention. I've decided there was nothing out there of much interest to her. It was just *her* time—time she didn't want to share.

"Outside the window on a cold January night back in 1930 a northeaster pounded away at the peace of that quiet street. The wind howled and roared its anger at the world and denied direction to swirling, lacy snowflakes, pushing one against the other in an effort to stop their inevitable descent."

"Mama stirred in her warm, safe bed. Had she been aroused by the fury demanding attention outside or by an urgent summons from within? Her gentle blue eyes opened wide. She sat up. Her heart pounded as she shook Daddy, asleep beside her, and whispered, 'It's time.' Daddy jumped out of bed and began to run from closet to bureau, to closet to bureau to closet to bureau. Mama watched shaking her head and smiling that special smile she reserved only for him. She waited patiently. Finally, ready to meet the crisis, Daddy stood by the side of their bed holding in his outstretched hand her shiny black, buckled overshoes. 'I'll need more than those.' she laughed.

"In spite of the storm's effort to frustrate their progress, perseverance eventually brought them to St. Mary's hospital. Long and laborious hours later, Dr. Emmerson looked down into those beautiful, smiling blue pools and said, 'You have a perfect little girl.' "

Emma pauses and breathes in the fresh mountain air. The purple finch has flown away, and the wind whistling through pines is all that can be heard. She looks down at her watch.

Lunch won't be served for awhile. She decides to go on.

"What do you think, Luke? Is it fate, luck or love that puts a smile on the face of survival?

"Mama said she and I were very lucky one unforgettable Saturday back in May of 1930. I was only five months old.

"As she told the story, the day began with the sun shining brightly through her kitchen windows. When the sun faded in the sky and the kitchen dimmed, she was not particularly concerned—a storm brewing. She wasn't aware black, billowing smoke had blocked out the sun. She didn't know a violent wind had begun to push a large, red-hot ball of fire down one street then another and that that flaming orb, started by a spark from the railroad tracks, had already haphazardly consumed everything in its path—trees, houses, garages, even the corner grocery store. It hadn't spared the beds, bureaus, chairs, tables, sofas and children's toys neighbors had frantically placed on vacant lots from homes feared were in the path of the uncontrolled predator. Tears came to Mama's eyes when she commented, 'They needn't have bothered.' You see, the rolling flames, bright, burning and laughing, had bounced over the empty homes onto the once-vacant lots.

"Uncle Danny and Blanche were coming to dinner that evening, and Mama had been busy setting her table and arranging a centerpiece with violets and pansies. She had stepped back to admire her handiwork when she heard the screams. The centerpiece and her glistening china, crystal and sterling silver flatware—ready for their debut—were quickly forgotten. Mama ran to the window and struggled to open it. When it finally gave way she leaned out as far as she dared and couldn't believe what was happening—neighbors, confused, were screaming and running in every direction. She turned and saw the huge ball of flames careening toward her. Paralyzed by fear, she somehow managed to get to my crib. She picked me up and rushed downstairs into the street where a cacophony of terror and confusion greeted and gripped her. She ran across the street and stood numb on the sidewalk. Her mind refused to function. All she could do was clutch me closer to her heart and let the tears flow freely from her beautiful blue eyes. Those eyes stared blankly as they watched flames hungrily consume her home and cherished wedding gifts—some still neatly nestled in their crisp, white tissue paper.

"She stood there in another world as the huge ball continued to roll and bounce in the wind, caring nought for the heartache its trail of flames had left behind.

"Daddy's familiar voice reached her above the sounds of human terror and the screeching of racing fire engines. She breathed a sigh of relief as she saw the one person she was praying to see, shove and push his way through the crowds. He frantically waved and yelled, 'Hannah, Hannah.' Still clutching me tightly, she ran toward him desperately shouting 'Chocolate, Chocolate. Oh, thank God. What'll we do? I left Emma's formula behind.' As he hugged us both, he looked across the street and saw the stairs on the right side of the building were still there. Reluctant to leave us, he warned Mama to stay where she was and rushed across the street bounding up the stairs two at a time. He burst into the kitchen, opened the icebox door and grabbed the bottles of formula. As he raced back to the door, he stopped. Mama's engagement ring peered up at him from the table. He stared at it and put the bottles down on the table. He quickly removed his watch—her wedding present to him—and laid it beside her ring. With tears in his eyes he grabbed the formula and hurried toward the stairs. But they were enveloped in flames and impossible to descend. Desperate, he jumped from the window, landing in a sitting position on the roof of his car, the bottles of formula clutched tightly in his hands.

"Many years later that leap changed all of our lives.

"When their world returned to normal, Daddy asked Mama why she had left her engagement ring on the kitchen table. She told him she didn't know. He confessed then that he had left his watch on the table beside her ring. When she asked him why, he also did not know. But as they sauntered through life like a couple of hoboes on a back-country road, they came to understand why two valuables burned together side by side on an unforgettable Saturday afternoon in May of 1930."

Emma gazes over at Luke, unmoved, staring into space. Quietly, she gets up and walks into the house.

Moments later, Catherine comes out onto the porch after having noticed Emma getting into the elevator. She approaches Luke and gently helps him up from his chair.

"Sure and it's just about time for lunch Luke me boy," she says as she guides him up to his room on the third floor.

Lying motionless on the bed, moored in his dark domain, Luke struggles with the old lady's intrusion into the quiet of his hidden realm. He mistrusts her invasive droning on and on.

I won't listen to her.

The next day brings a cooler breeze. Emma, Luke and a few other hardy souls are enjoying the warmth of afghans spread across their knees.

Buoyed by the exhilarating air, Emma crosses the fingers of both hands and begins, "Good morning, Luke. I hope you slept well."

She looks at the sad figure sitting beside her, and though she doesn't expect a response, Emma feels just a bit let down.

"I've got a question this morning, and I think the answer will make a pretty good story.

"What's more important? Where we've been or where we're going?

"Where was I the first five years of my life? I don't remember.

"One of the first things I can recall is an apartment on Beech Street where Mr. Nelson delivered groceries in an old green wagon pulled by a horse that looked as ancient and weary as he did.

"A few other things stand out—wonderful stories of times before mine; piggy-back rides on strong, broad shoulders; hugs for no reason; smiles just because; sheets warmed in the oven on cold winter nights; large, fluffy, white towels easing disappointment at the end of a frolicking bath; picnics of tuna fish sandwiches, small gherkin pickles and ice cold milk; silver slides that were high, low and curved; swings that went to the sky and mud pies frosted with sparkling yellow dandelions.

"Mama's lap, warm and comfy, was the perfect place to listen to stories about me. Her favorite was my favorite too.

"How did it go? Let's see, something like, 'When you were

only three, on a bright, starlit evening, I put you down into your warm crib-bed, which Daddy and I had placed by the window so you could watch the world go by. I tucked the pink and white quilt, scattered with your favorite bears and squirrels, under your chin. We said our prayers, and I kissed your nose then tiptoed toward the door. As I was about to leave, I turned and blew you a kiss. You called, 'Mama.' I came back and heard you say, as you pointed to the sky, 'The lights are on in heaven.'

"Mothers have wonderful stories to tell.

"It's strange, but I remember that crib-bed. I've never seen another one like it. Painted a light green, it was about the size of a twin bed but had slatted sides. I think Grampy, Daddy's father, made it, but I'm not sure of that.

"Gram, Mama's mother, loved to tell me how, when I came to visit as a really little girl, I had to sleep on a daybed in her dining room. In the morning, Gramps would come through on his way to the kitchen. He'd always stop, if I happened to be awake, and say, 'I'm going to eat you, Emma.' Gram would laugh remembering my answer, 'Not today Gramps.'

"Fathers have stories too. I love the one Daddy used to tell when I asked why he had to leave each morning. It was a wonderful tale about cutting dried animal skins into many varied shapes and sizes. The skins were placed on a cart and wheeled into a large room with noisy machines. The machines sewed the different shapes together, and they eventually wound up as shoes to put on my little feet so they'd be well protected when I went out to roller skate, jump rope or play hopscotch.

"And then there were stories about the winters he bundled

me up in my one-piece snowsuit, scarf and hat and snapped brown, rubber overshoes tightly around my ankles. We left Mama at the shed door wringing her hands and begging us not to go. But, mittened hand in mittened hand, we waded out into a blowing northeaster to make the first footprints in snow flakes landing, one upon the other, trying to climb back to the sky from which they were descending.

"How patient he was when he tried to teach me to snowplow and make a stem christy on my first pair of tiny wood skis with only leather straps for bindings. And no less patient when he tried so hard to teach me to dive. But I never could put my head in the water first.

"Thanksgiving was Daddy's favorite holiday. He always took Mama and me to the movies after dinner. They were married on Thanksgiving Day, and he insisted on celebrating no matter what the date.

"Was I only eight when we moved to Baxter Street? Or was I ten? I'm not sure. Anyway, it's there I see Mama so vividly standing at her white-enameled gas stove (with two ovens on top). Many hours of her life were spent at that stove preparing pot roast, fricassee chicken, strawberry shortcake, lemon pies and cookies that looked like farmyard animals. If she wasn't cooking, her small frame would be bent over a gray, soapstone sink as sheets, towels, blouses and socks traveled up and down a metal-ribbed washboard on their journey to the clothesline in the back yard. Later, from the window, I watched as she tried to retrieve the billowing sheets being blown over her head of tangled curls by a cold north wind. How she would laugh. And how I loved that melodious, happy sound. At Christmas time it rang out like silver bells.

"We always spent Christmas in Canfield about twelve miles north of Collier where Gram and Gramps lived in a large, white apartment house across the bridge from the center of town. It was hardly visible sitting quietly behind a huge, ancient elm tree.

"The whole family gathered there—even aunts, uncles and cousins from as far away as Massachusetts.

"When Gram announced Santa would be arriving soon, my cousins and I would run to her cold living-room window where we waited and watched. When I think of it, even to this day, I can feel my little body stiffen and my eyes open wide as Santa appeared out of the swirling, blinding snow in his bright red suit trimmed with fluffy white fur. He trudged across the bridge toward us—snow up to the top of his shiny black boots, a bag of gifts riding high upon his shoulders. Pushing snowflakes out of his way, he came nearer and nearer. I watched until I heard his footsteps on the stairs leading up to Gram's apartment, then ran frightened and crying into Daddy's knees. Years seemed to go by waiting for that knock, knock, knock. When it came, Daddy scooped me up and took me into Gram's bedroom, where he held me tight as we listened to Santa's loud and jolly, "Ho. Ho. Ho." along with the clapping, giggles, "Oooo." and "Ahhh." of those gathered around the Christmas tree. When the Ho, Ho, Hos were still and Daddy had convinced me Santa'd gone upon his merry way, we slowly opened the door, and I'd run to see what had been left for me.

"Many a Christmas came and went before I found out Uncle Harry had been Santa Claus. How tickled he must have been when I ran to him yelling he'd missed Santa. I never thought it strange that he always arrived just minutes before Gram served her Christmas dinner. We weren't as smart then as kids are today."

Emma has been watching Luke hoping for something, anything, if only a small twitch in his pale, expressionless cheek.

She prays he's wrestling with the loss of his own childhood memories, for it's important the wrestling begin.

Santa Claus? Swings? Towels? Tuna Fish? Snow? Sit somewhere else lady. Just leave me alone.

Rain returns to the mountains and continues to water the earth for the next four days. A quiet stillness within the house contrasts the pelting torrents assaulting its defending windowpanes.

Luke is nowhere to be seen. Emma, if not reading, spends her time in the chapel.

But, today, the sun shines warm and comforting. Emma and Luke can be seen at the far end of the wide front porch.

"What a glorious morning, Luke. Can you feel how warm the sun is?"

There is no reply.

Emma's faith prevails.

"Life's journey never rests, does it?"

Emma rocks and the floorboards respond.

"The clock ticked away year after year. When was it I began to feel a difference? Oh, I guess I was probably six or seven years old.

"Smiles were no longer there "just because."

"Something had happened in the grown-up world. Daddy was the same but somehow different. The sparkle in Mama's eyes had dimmed. I wondered why. But I didn't dwell on it, because what was happening in my childish world was far more important.

"Then came that unforgettable Saturday morning. Mama and I had just finished breakfast when she leaned across the table and took my hand in hers. As gently as she knew how, she told me she would not be home when I returned from school on Monday afternoon. She was going to be a telephone operator at Perkins & Company where she had worked before she married Daddy.

"Then she told me something had happened to Daddy's legs and the doctors couldn't help him. They didn't know the what or the why. She tried to explain that at times, mostly at night, his legs would shake violently and at other times he'd lose his balance just stepping on a small pebble.

"I hadn't noticed.

"The doctors advised Mama to find a job since they couldn't predict how much longer Daddy would be able to work at the shoe factory.

"I know it must have been very difficult for her to smile. But she did and asked if I understood. I didn't understand, and I couldn't smile; I just stared and squeezed her hand. I closed my eyes and saw Daddy jump from a flaming window. I saw him fly through the air with bottles of my formula held high over his head. To this day that image haunts me.

"Mama continued to hold my hand and listened while I repeated the story of Daddy's crazy nickname. I loved the story 'cause it always made me laugh, and I wanted to match Mama's courageous smile.

"Daddy was seven years old when he worked down in the cellar of a grocery store where he transferred potatoes from a large wooden barrel into peck, brown-paper bags. Members of his neighborhood gang helped him after Daddy bribed them with small chocolate cakes he'd taken from one of the counters upstairs. Poor Mr. O'Brien, he couldn't figure out why his chocolate cakes were disappearing, until the day he caught Daddy sneaking down the back stairs—his pockets bulging. Mr. O'Brien gave his little ears a good boxing and from that day on called him Chocolate."

"I couldn't manage that smile.

"I asked Mama if he was going to die. She assured me his life was not in danger. I asked if he'd have to be in a wheelchair. As gently as she could, she told me it was very possible that some day he would not be able to walk.

"No one was going to tell Chocolate he would never place his foot upon the earth again. Each night after dinner he'd say, 'C'mon,' and we would walk, his arm clutching mine, for two blocks, no matter what the weather. After all, no northeaster ever blew that was too much of a challenge for him and me. He never complained of the pain. In fact he never said anything at all. It was just one foot in front of the other. Oh, I knew the pain was there; I could see it in his eyes, and I can still feel his involuntary squeeze on my arm.

"Sheer willpower kept him from ever having to push the large, awkward orbs of a wheelchair. He had such unbelievable determination. He worked on and off for many years in spite of the pain and continued to ski the slopes of these mountains he loved so much. Perhaps not as often, nor as fast, nor on expert trails, but he skied nevertheless.

"During the summer, on his good days, he played golf—his game of games. How he hated playing only nine holes and riding in a cart. But absolutely nothing could crush his pride.

"A disability interfere with the adventures life offered Chocolate? Never."

Emma's voice disappears into the rhythmical "Squeak. Squeak. Squeak."

Catherine has stolen a few minutes to listen to Emma's story. She looks at Luke's blank face and then at Emma. She tries to comfort Emma with an encouraging smile before hurrying off. As she disappears through the front door, she waves to Marie coming out onto the porch.

Why must she go on and on?

It's such a beautiful day Emma asks Marie if she'd mind serving her lunch out on the porch.

Marie smiles, "No problem, Mrs. Duprey."

Catherine returns and takes Luke to his room where she finds it easier to assist him with his meals. Emma is left alone until Marie leaves a tuna fish sandwich and a cup of hot spiced tea on her wicker table.

"Enjoy. See you later."

Emma's teenage years promenade through the refreshing September air as she eats and rocks contentedly, wondering where to begin their story when Catherine returns with Luke. Why not that dreadful day she walked up Main Street to begin her freshman year at Collier High?

Deep in thought, Emma isn't aware of Marie removing the empty dishes. For no apparent reason, as Marie reaches the front door, she pauses and looks back at Emma. At the same moment, Catherine and Luke step out onto the porch, and the three collide. Marie is dismayed when her tray crashes to the floor. Startled, Emma turns. Catherine yells to her, "No problem Emma, everything's okay. Sure and it's just a wee collision. Everybody's fine. C'mon Luke let's join Emma—just a few more steps."

Seemingly unruffled, Luke sits quietly in his chair.

With a smile in her voice, Emma remarks, "Well, a little excitement never hurt anyone. Kind of perks up the day."

Marie and Catherine quickly dispose of the tray and the broken dishes before Catherine returns to make sure Emma and Luke are all right.

"Don't worry about us, Catherine, we're both fine. I was just about to ask Luke to consider this question. If life wasn't such a mystery, do you think any of us would venture forth?"

"Sure and I'll have to think about that one, Emma? You're positive you're okay?

Emma nods and Catherine hurries off.

"I can tell you, Luke, if I'd known what lay ahead for me that day after Labor Day many years ago, I would never have left my bed.

"A new red plaid dress lay on top of the bedspread. On the floor sat a pair of highly polished brown loafers sporting bright copper pennies.

"It was my first day of high school. I sat on the window seat that morning enchanted by maple leaves turning to gold in the bright sunlight. But the aroma of bacon brought me back to reality and the clock told me I`d better hurry.

"I put on my new dress and slid into the shoes with shiny copper pennies. The mirror suggested I redo my hair. I remember feeling disappointed as I pulled the brush through it. Somehow, I didn't look quite the way I'd planned, but time wouldn't allow for fussing. I ran down stairs into the kitchen. Mama told me I looked lovely. In her eyes I guess I did. Thankfully, she didn't insist I eat breakfast—only a glass of orange juice.

"I know Mama felt my dread and hated pointing to the clock hanging on the wall above the refrigerator. I gulped down the juice, but my legs wouldn't move. She kissed my cheek and pushed me out the door. Half way down the porch steps I turned around and tried to smile. Mama, standing behind the screen door, rushed out and gave me what she hoped was a comforting hug as she insisted I'd be fine.

"It was a long walk up to the high school on Canton Street, a long walk that suited me just fine; I wasn't in any hurry. I strolled up Main Street, satchel hanging from my shoulder, and peered into the store windows along the way. They all reflected a young girl in a red plaid dress pushing her long hair behind her ears, thinking that maybe her mother had been right after all.

"As each sparkling pane lost its animation, I became preoccupied with happier times at the parochial school I'd attended for the past nine years. Its building was old and comfortable; the nuns kind and familiar. I reminisced about Sister Catherine, who taught the fourth grade; she was a bit of a terror at times. I smiled thinking about my fifth grade teacher, Sister Martha, who, on Fridays, would let us bring in records and dance away the last hour of the afternoon.

"I looked up and gasped, 'Oh no. Not so soon.' The street sign read Canton Street. I had arrived, and there it was— Collier High School.

"A large white sign with red letters one couldn't miss had been placed strategically in the middle of a plush green lawn. It read A through M register at Gym—N through Z register at Auditorium. Which was which? I chose the doors to the right; my prayers were answered—for awhile. When I gave my name to the stern looking teacher seated at a table scanning names listed alphabetically, she said it wasn't on her sheet and advised me to try the auditorium. I wasn't on that sheet either and ended up standing in the doorway of the main office on the first floor. Behind a long counter holding up several obviously bored students, an exhausted looking man—tall, slim, with bushy, black eyebrows and no hair—called out to me, 'Are you sure you've been promoted?' I can almost taste the tears that crept down my cheeks like raindrops on a rose petal. Of course I'd been promoted.

"The question of my promotion was finally settled and I was given a schedule of classes and the number of my homeroom. The man with no hair pointed to the door and out I walked making my way in strange surroundings filled with a sea of unknown faces.

"My first period geometry class was almost over when I arrived. Mr. Ericson did not look pleased and gruffly assigned me a front seat in the third row. I now occupied the only front seat in the classroom. Behind me sat twenty or more ill mannered, snickering males. Mr. Ericson went directly to a strange looking telephone hanging on the wall by the door. He told whoever was on the other end that he did not want a girl in his class. I found myself again facing the exhausted looking man with bushy eyebrows. He assigned me to a Miss Ashley's geometry class. When I walked into her room, needless to say she was not pleased either, since the dismissal bell had just rung. I apologized for being late and returned to the unfriendly hallways in search of freshman English.

"I finally reached the last hour of the day, a study period with Mr. Correlli, the assistant football coach. Again male heads turned as I walked through the door. I suppose most girls would have been thrilled. But I wasn't most girls—not then. Mr. Correlli told me to find a seat.

"At exactly 2:33 PM the closing bell of the day rang and off I went, pushing my way through the crowded hallways until I reached the fresh air. I raced down Canton Street onto Main Street, speeding past the store windows, caring less about their reflections. All that mattered was getting home; I had a message for Mama. When I reached the back porch, I snatched the key from its hiding place in the pot of geraniums and opened the door. I dropped my satchel and books on the table with a bang then walked immediately over to the telephone and dialed. I heard Mama say, 'Perkins & Company.' Waiting perhaps a half a second, in a tone not angry, determined is the better word, I announced, 'I'm never going back there. No matter what you say, Mama, I'm not going back.'

"But of course I did. And old friends helped me make new ones."

Emma rocks. The floorboards sing their song. She looks at Luke and wonders what, if anything, is going on behind that blank face.

She doesn't know, might never know. But tomorrow, if the weather holds, she'll continue.

Please, please lady, whoever you are, just buzz off.

The next morning familiar figures rock back and forth, back and forth along the wide, circular porch absorbing the pleasurable warmth radiated by a sun smiling and shining on the mountains. It's a happy sun this morning—no one is missing.

Of course one chair is not rocking. But what matter—a mind can listen, ponder and wrestle whether moving or perfectly still.

"Churlee. Churlee. Churlee"

Again, thc purple finch competes with Emma's soft, melodious voice.

"Well, Luke, I hope you're enjoying this wonderful mountain air as much as I am."

He offers no competition to the little purple bird.

"I've been sitting here thinking how each crisis we face builds courage for another that will surely follow.

"I was only sixteen when my first crisis came along.

"Shyness had forever been my torment. But it seemed to loosen its grip as I went to football games and basketball games and suffered through crushes on athletic heroes. I even went to the Y on Saturday nights and watched friends dance in a trance to *My Old Flame.* I wasn't a star at the Y like I was in the classroom—which strangely enough happened to be one of my favorite places.

"Stars on the dance floor don't wear braces on their teeth. Stars on the dance floor aren't five feet six inches tall weighing only ninety-eight pounds. I did have pretty brown hair though. But it was turning white. As long as I can remember Chocolate had always had white hair, and Grammie's had turned by the time she was twenty-three.

"Back in the forties if you wanted to change the color of your hair, your choices were jet black, brassy red or bleach blond—none of which appealed to me. By the time I reached twenty-nine, the top of my head resembled a snow-capped mountain. But, I certainly had a long way to go before reaching that ancient age.

"Hair color was the last thing I was thinking of the night my friend Anne and I, blossoming freshmen, joined the crowd and marched up Main Street behind the high-school band toward Hatcher Stadium. We were going to our first football game. What a thrill it was marching into the lighted stadium and scrambling up into the bleachers to find a seat—never expecting the explosion that burst forth when Collier's white and gold ran out onto the field. We cheered until our throats went dry. Anne and I were hooked. Not on football, at least not I. Good heavens, I've never been able to figure out what's going on. No, we wanted to be cheerleaders.

"When our sophomore year rolled around, Anne made the squad, but I didn't have the courage to try out. You needed confidence to be a cheerleader, and, outside the classroom, I was a bit wanting in that department. But my desire never waned, and Anne kept encouraging me.

"Junior year arrived like an unexpected relative on the front stoop. Once more it was time for cheerleader tryouts.

"I asked myself where my sophomore year had gone and what had happened to my plans to practice, practice, practice? Somehow they'd just disappeared. And with them my courage. Another opportunity lost.

"Time flew by. Spring arrived, and the school corridors were alive with excitement over the upcoming prom. Like all springs, tiny buds miraculously appeared on lifeless tree limbs. Suddenly the grass was green, and cement sidewalks rumbled under laughing youngsters on roller skates.

"No one invited me to the prom, but that was no surprise. Boys never paid much attention to timid, plain Emma.

"The big day dawned like any other but developed quite unexpectedly.

"It all started in the middle of a second-period Latin class, where I was struggling with a quiz on the fall of the Roman Empire. I can hear Miss Green's whisper in my ear as if it were yesterday, 'You're wanted down in Miss Cooper's office.'

"I was surprised to see Anne and two other friends in the waiting room. When I arrived, we were asked to come in and sit down. We did so staring quizzically at each other. Miss Cooper smiled across her desk and told us she had been asked to represent four junior boys who wanted to take the four of us to the prom that evening. She added they were very shy and didn't have the courage to ask us themselves. We stared at each other again, but this time unbelievingly. Then we started to babble excitedly that we couldn't possibly go on such short notice. Miss Cooper tried to impress upon us how important it was to the boys' self-esteem that we accept their invitations. But she never did share how she knew the boys wanted to ask us. Had their counselor convinced them that we would be devastated if we didn't attend our first prom? We knew all four martyrs and were totally humiliated at what they must have thought. Although Miss Cooper continued her efforts to convince us, her powers of persuasion failed her. We returned to our classes dumbfounded and speechless. At lunch we could talk of nothing else and were so thankful that none of the boys were in our afternoon sessions.

"During my last-period study, Mr. Peterson responded to a knock on the door and turned to say I was wanted in the corridor. Hector, the brain of my Latin class, stood in front of Miss Green and asked if I would go to the prom with him that evening. I was about to refuse, when I noticed the look on Miss Green's face. It seemed to convey the message that if I didn't say yes I could expect an F in Latin. I might have misinterpreted that look. But being unwilling to gamble, I accepted Hector's invitation.

"When I returned to my seat, Mr. Peterson informed me I was free to leave. As I walked down the hallway, a caldron of angry bubbles roiled and boiled inside me. I looked up and saw Amy and Connie. I yelled, "Oh no, you too?" From around the corner came Anne. We'd all had the same experience.

"Furious, we sat on the stairs at the end of the corridor trying to think rationally. We agreed gowns had to be our first priority. But we didn't have enough time, or money, to go shopping. We sat silently, chins in our hands, staring into space. All of a sudden Anne jumped up and blurted out, 'My sisters' old gowns. Pattie, Maggie and Ellie won't care if we wear them. They wouldn't be caught dead in a gown they'd worn before.'

"Wow, what an inspiration. The four of us simultaneously raced down the stairs and out the front door. We ran home with Anne and followed her up the stairs into the attic. She pulled open the door of an immense closet, and, with a bravado wave of her arm, revealed its contents. Amy, Connie and I stared with open mouths. Before us was a wardrobe that could have been waiting for the cast of the Ziegfeld Follies. We tried on every gown hanging there. What a wonderful time we had. For a few, fun moments we forgot why we had come.

"I fell in love with the most beautiful dress I had ever seen. It was light blue, shimmering with layers and layers of rhinestone-studded netting. All I could think of was a fairy mountain reflecting the stars. I held it up in front of me and whirled around the attic—just for a moment I was the star of Swan Lake.

"Unfortunately, like all the others, it was too short. But I refused to relinquish my dream dress hoping Mama could somehow make it longer.

"As soon as I arrived home, I telephoned her and explained what had happened. There was silence on the other end of the line. Impatient, I demanded, 'Mama, can you lengthen the dress?'

"'Give me a minute,' she said.

"I could hear her thinking, 'I can darn socks, fix rips and sew on buttons, but lengthen a ball gown?'

"'Of course,' she exclaimed, 'Aunt Lena.' She told me to wait a minute and not to worry; she'd call me right back. I sat down by the telephone staring at the fairy mountain and wondered why this had to happen to me.

"Mama called Aunt Lena, who lived in Canfield across the bridge from Gram. She told Mama to send me up on the next bus.

"I was jolted from my reverie when Mama called and told me to catch the next bus to Canfield. With the dress folded over my arm, the skirt billowing in the wind, I ran as fast as I could. Thank goodness the bus station was just down the street.

"Aunt Lena was at the door waiting for me. She wasted no time. I watched in awe—her hands almost invisible they moved so fast. I'll never know how, but she managed to get the dress down to my ankles. Not ideal, but a lot better than it was. When she finished ironing it, she carefully wrapped it in tissue paper and placed it in a large white box. I kissed her on the cheek and raced down the street to catch the last bus back to Collier, all the while trying desperately to hang onto that large, white box.

"On the trip home, I stared out the window thinking about all the different fellows Miss Cooper could have chosen for me. My thoughts suddenly switched like tracks in a train yard.

"'Shoes, good grief, shoes.'

"The stores would be closed when I got home. I began to panic. My shoes were going to show. Maybe Mama had a pair I could wear. Oh, but my feet were much bigger than hers. I had no choice. I would have to wear my black suede flats; they were the dressiest pair I owned.

"Time tormented me. I arrived home just one hour before doomsday. Mama and I did our best to make a young lady going to her first prom feel and look like a young lady going to her first prom. We both knew we had failed. Daddy said I looked beautiful just seconds before Hector rang the doorbell.

"I'm not going to dwell on the rest of the evening. We all survived. After Hector left, and before I went inside to answer all the questions I knew were on the tip of Mama's tongue, I stood on the front steps and looked up into the sky sparkling with trillions and trillions of stars. Standing there I warned the Blessed Mother, 'If I don't go to the senior prom with someone of my own choice, I shall leave the church.'

"Mama greeted me with a look I'm sure she thought was well hidden. I assured her I'd had a wonderful time.

"Never in my wildest imagination did I think I would ever retrieve such a doleful memory to tell as an amusing and colorful story...which I did on a number of occasions.

"The prom was over. Everyone now looked forward with great expectation to the final assembly of our junior year. No one ever skipped school that day. Everyone wanted to hear the results of their votes for junior and senior class officers and committees.

"I certainly attended; I'd been nominated for the office of Secretary of the Senior Class—it almost made up for the junior prom.

"I can't possibly describe the torture I went through that day. Why the name of the Senior Class Secretary had to be the last one called is beyond me. The list of candidates that year was at least two miles long, but I was still in good health when my name was finally read.

"A summer of fun lay ahead, but I had to answer an important question—just how badly did I want to be a cheerleader? Time was running out. It was now or never. I made up my mind.

"What a summer it turned out to be. One or two hours a day, every day, I practiced the entire cheer repertoire of the Collier High cheerleading squad—if at home, out in the barn, if away, wherever I could find space and solitude. My commitment could only be compared to that of the riders of the Pony Express.

"When September rolled around, my limbs moved like a well oiled engine. My voice projected so far an eagle listening high atop its aerie would have no choice but to answer my call and add its own special sound to the roar resounding below. I finally felt the confidence I needed, and I had no doubt I would be the best cheerleader Collier High ever had."

Emma pauses and looks over at Luke. His eyelids blink—a natural happening he can't prevent. Thick, black hair sweeps his brow as a breeze disturbs the afternoon stillness.

Why the hell am I listening?

Emma feels a strange presence and turns her head. An unfamiliar visitor is leaning against the railing a few feet away. Emma instinctively knows she has been listening. The attractive, expensively dressed woman doesn't move but seems to be waiting as she looks over at Emma and Luke. Emma gets up and walks slowly toward her. Who else could she be but Luke's mother?

"Good afternoon, my name's Emma."

"Good afternoon, I am Luke's mother. My name is Margaret, but everyone, including my son, calls me Muffin."

She adds with a smile, "Why? I cannot tell you."

"I'd like to call you Margaret."

Luke's mother nods and smiles.

"Would you like to join me in the parlor, Margaret?"

Margaret nods again and follows Emma into a lovely room furnished with antique tables, chairs and sofas. Ancient landscapes in chipped, antique-gold frames adorn the walls—all treasures left behind by appreciative families of former residents.

Marie comes in.

"Ah, Marie, do you suppose we could have some tea? Would you also check to see if there are any macaroons left?"

Marie, who is very, very fond of Emma, smiles and bows her head.

"I'm sure there are some tucked away in the kitchen somewhere Mrs. Duprey."

Margaret, sitting on the edge of her chair, watches Marie leave and then turns to smile at Emma.

"Catherine told me what you are trying to do for my son. I must thank you for your kind effort and concern, but I am quite convinced there is nothing more anyone can do for him. Luke has been here almost six months. I had hoped he would gather strength from the mountains—at least enough to want to write his music again. He wrote beautiful music you know, when he was not off on that dreadful motorcycle. I am afraid a great deal more than sight and memory has been taken from him."

"I didn't know about his music."

"My son has heard notes all his life. He started writing them down when he was about five. He has never been able to endure losing even one. I think of him as my musical miser. But he has never shared his music with me."

"Margaret—"

"Before you say anything more, Emma, I must tell you that I am going to take Luke home today."

Emma's panic almost chokes her, but she has lived long enough to know she mustn't lose control. She smiles and gently asks Margaret, "Would you mind telling me a little bit more about Luke?"

Before Margaret can answer, Marie returns with a lovely yellow, gold-rimmed teapot, two matching teacups and a plate of macaroons. She places her tray down on the table in front of Emma. Smiling warmly, she tells Emma to ring if she needs anything else and quietly leaves the room.

As Emma pours the tea, she asks, "Is Luke an only child?"

Still perched on the edge of her chair Margaret accepts the tea and responds, "No, he is the youngest of my three boys."

Surprised, Emma hesitates.

"Really, oh my, I had him pictured alone in a huge mansion, rich and spoiled. I've truly become quite fond of Luke but know so little about him. Please tell me more about his music. I'm also curious about how he fit into your family life and where he went to school. What did he enjoy reading? What kinds of food does he prefer? Oh my, I'm sorry, Margaret, for bombarding you with so many questions—but one more, please. He looks like his father doesn't he? I ask because of your blond hair and lovely blue eyes."

Emma sees something besides sadness in those eyes. She detects a desire to share with someone a hidden emotional turmoil.

"Would you mind also telling me a little something about yourself Margaret?"

Margaret takes a sip of her tea and settles back against the cushions of her chair.

"Luke never really wanted to be a part of our family, all of whom are Boston born and bred.

"And yes, you are correct. He looks like Edward. My husband is a very highly intelligent and respected heart surgeon. He graduated from Harvard and its Medical School. Ah, my dear Edward, he is such a kind and caring human being.

"As for myself, I went to Wellesley College and have never been anything but a wife and mother since I graduated. My husband and my boys have been my life. It is as simple as that.

"My two older sons are lawyers and very happily married. I have two handsome grandsons and an adorable little granddaughter. One should not ask for more."

Margaret leans forward and places her teacup on the coffee table. She looks over at Emma before settling back comfortably in the chair.

"But then there is Luke…and so I do ask for more. But not in the way you might think.

"Luke has always hated the way we live. He says we exist in a world of our own, refusing to accept reality, afraid it will somehow soil us. He says we are puppets high on a pedestal, perfect, untouchable, totally controlled by our society. Even though he lived in the same house, he never seemed a member of the family. If we all dressed for dinner, Luke would wear jeans, a T-shirt and sneakers—not necessarily clean ones—if he came at all.

"Sometimes during thunder and lightening storms he would go off on his motorcycle, not seeming to care that I stood frightened at the front door.

"When he came back, he would laugh at me insisting I should not worry about him…that his notes, hidden by the thunder, had been out there somewhere dancing in the rain waiting for him. It never made any sense to me, but I would smile as though I understood.

"We have never been able to talk, he and I. Now we probably never will.

"No, Emma, he did not go beyond high school.

"What does he like to eat? I do not know.

"Did he read? I hope so.

"Although he would not play for me, once in awhile I would hear enchanting, lovely sounds coming from some distant part of the house. I knew it was Luke playing his guitar. But the music was so inconsistent with his lifestyle. I have listened to him and his friends out in the garage and what I have heard could not, by any stretch of the imagination, be called music.

"Sometimes I wonder if there might be two of him. I would like to think there is. You see I have a plan. I want to take the "real" Luke away to a cottage on an island somewhere off the eastern seaboard or maybe a log cabin higher up in these mountains. I want to take care of him. I want him to need and depend on me.

"Once in a while, in order to give me time to go home and search for his music, I plan to call Catherine and ask her to stay with him for a day or two, if we are settled around here. If we end up living on an island, I'd have to find someone else.

"You see, Emma, his music is the key. I am sure of it, and I must find it. If I am successful, I will have a guitarist record the music so Luke and I can sit by the ocean, or on a mountain peak, wherever we happen to be, and listen, just listen, dreaming our own separate dreams.

"When I sense a change in the way he is listening, I will give him his guitar. He will play. I know he will play. Dr. Billings tried having him listen to music and even put his guitar on his lap. But Luke never responded. He would not have, because it was not *his* music. I am convinced that if he hears his own notes he will want to play them.

"I know it sounds unrealistic, Emma, perhaps a bit desperate, but he should at least have his music. And I want to be the one to give it back to him. The others really do not need me anymore."

Emma leans over and pats Margaret's hand.

"No, Margaret, you don't want to isolate your son. You mustn't give up hope. You just said to me, 'When I *sense* a change in the way he is listening…' Well, I have *sensed* for awhile now that progress is being made. He should have far more than just his music. Can there be any harm in letting me have a few more weeks with him? I want to give him a future so that when he is as old as I am he'll have a past to reflect upon."

Margaret gazes at the woman she sees as old and senile.

Emma, old but far from senile, continues, "Are there overt signs of Luke responding? No! But I know, somehow, that he's listening to my stories sitting there day after day." She reaches out to take Margaret's hand.

Margaret immediately reaches for her tea cup.

Emma smiles. "A minuscule hope, perhaps, but it's there for me. Can it be for you?"

Margaret turns her head to look out the window.

Who is she anyway? She certainly thinks she is helping, poor dear. I suppose it makes her feel needed…and I suppose I should be more charitable. Another week will not make much difference.

She smiles at Emma and says, "I suppose I could wait one more week."

Emma's panic subsides and she smiles her thanks. Margaret returns her smile before getting up to go out onto the porch to join her son. Emma relaxes on the sofa for a few more minutes then rises and walks wearily toward the elevator with the thought of spending a few minutes in the chapel. Wandering down the hallway of the second floor, she wonders if she has enough strength to push open the chapel door. She does. As she enters and kneels down, thunder begins to rumble. She knows rain will soon be rapping on the windowpanes. The stained-glass image of her Maker, serene in the window above the altar, holds her attention.

"Thank You. But a week?"

A streak of lightening splits the sky in two before thunder roars its revelation.

Emma's heart skips a beat.

"Is that all the time *I* have? Oh My! Well, I'll certainly do the best I can. Now don't desert me."

The following morning, before going down to breakfast, Emma searches for a three-ring binder—an old friend from long ago. After going through the drawers of both bureaus, she remembers there's a large box under the bed. Ignoring her arthritic back, she pushes the box away from its hiding place with the help of Uncle Harry's old shillelagh. She hurries around the bed and stops—perplexed. The box looks so tired and sad. How did it get that tattered and worn?

Willingly enduring the pain, Emma bends down to remove the cover. As she carefully lifts it from its timeworn resting place, the cover seems to slump into her loving hands. She peers into the box. Sitting on top of many other forgotten treasures, the three-ring binder seems to return her soft, small smile. Emma lifts it up and slowly rises leaning heavily on the bedpost. Pressing the binder to her heart, she sits down by the window and stares lovingly at her old friend. With near reverence she flips through its pages and savors the memories they hold.

"I hope my fingers are strong enough to pull open your rings."

It takes a little effort, but Emma finds the strength. She removes the page she has been searching for and tucks it into the pocket of her sweater. Carefully, so as not to pinch her fingers, she snaps the rings shut.

"Now where shall I put you? I'll be needing you again. Ah, of course, you'll fit perfectly right here on my little table. I should have brought you out a long time ago."

Emma rises and walks toward the door. As she is about to close it she looks back and enjoys a comforting warmth at the sight of her binder on the table by her chair.

Later, as she steps out of the elevator, she sees Marie crossing the foyer and calls out to her, "Marie, would you mind doing me a favor?"

"Sure, if I can, Mrs. Duprey."

"When you're up on the second floor would you go into my room and put the big box by the side of my bed back under the bed? I didn't want to use any more of my energy putting it back. Thank you dear, I would appreciate it."

"No problem."

Luke has been sitting quietly in his rocker unaware of Emma standing in the doorway absorbing the strength of Mount Washington. She looks over at him before beginning her daily stroll around the porch. Taking her time, she inhales the invigorating morning air. As she approaches her chair she stops and stares at the back of Luke's handsome head. Squeezing the piece of paper in her pocket, Emma says a silent prayer and sits down to begin the closing of her teenage years.

"How are you this morning, Luke? You look fine. I wish you would tell me that you're fine.

Oh how I wish, how I wish.

As if thinking out loud Emma begins.

"I see a daisy in its meadow swaying to the rhythm of the wind. It doesn't see the reaper come. When laid upon its side, it weeps and feels alone."

Emma hopes Luke catches the meaning of her words.

"I couldn't wait for Labor Day and the start of my senior year. You see I knew in my heart I was now well prepared to try out for the squad. Anne couldn't wait for the other cheerleaders to see my expertise. But a polio epidemic dashed my enthusiasm. All school openings in the city were delayed until further notice.

"On the day that should have been my first as an exalted senior, Aunt Lena called to say she and Uncle Emory wanted to tour the White Mountains for a few days. She asked if I'd baby sit the funeral home's telephone, a telephone that could never, ever, under any circumstance, be left unattended. I was happy to. Aunt Lena had always come through for me.

"I gulped down my orange juice and grabbed a piece of toast before running off to catch the next bus to Canfield. As soon as I arrived, Aunt Lena and Uncle Emory left. I knew there'd be plenty of good food in the refrigerator and my kind of music stored in the back of the record cabinet.

"Downstairs the keys of the organ were covered. Mahogany, steel and cloth-covered caskets stood empty. The floorboards were silent—not creaking like they did when Uncle Emory pushed a heavy burden across them. Not even his new carpeting could silence their groans.

"The only sound came from an ancient Chauncy Boardman clock on its shelf in the front hallway.

"I went into the spare bedroom with my suitcase and smiled at the large, golden sunflowers grinning at me from a jersey Aunt Lena had put on the bed as a surprise. Out of its neckline peeked a pair of bright yellow socks, obviously purchased to match the sunflowers. Aunt Lena knew how much I loved yellow. I immediately put both on before retrieving *The Count of Monte Cristo* from my suitcase. Back in the living room I snuggled into Aunt Lena's most comfortable armchair and let my colorful feet dangled over one arm.

"As Frank Sinatra sang *Stardust,* I continued the story that has always been my favorite, even after all these years. I had just finished reading the part where Edmond Dantes, who had been imprisoned in the Chateau D'If for so many wasted years, was about to escape. The telephone rang just as he was thrown into the sea.

"I leaped out of the chair thinking good grief, who's died? When I answered, 'Emory T. Brown & Son.' Mama didn't even say hello, just, 'Emma hurry and catch the next bus to Collier and get up to the high school as fast as you can. Anne called to let you know the first football game of the season is going to be played on schedule, and there will be no time for cheerleader tryouts. Two uniforms have been assigned and there's one left. Don't worry about the telephone sweetheart. Lock the door and run.'

"Oh my, did I race down to the Rexall drugstore, arriving just as the door of the bus to Collier was about to close. How I waved and shouted to Joe to wait. He did.

"As the bus roared toward Collier, I concentrated on all the green leaves just beginning to think about turning red and yellow. I watched myself among the leaves dressed in a faded pair of green shorts and tan jersey struggling to perfect the cheers. As I continued to stare, the trees became Hatcher Stadium. 'Go team go,' I cheered dressed in a white flannel, gold-lined circular skirt beneath a white flannel jacket fastened with frogs of bright gold braiding. I wanted to shout, 'Joe, let's go. Why did you pick today to drive so slowly?'

"To ease my anxiety, I tried to concentrate on Daddy's smile of encouragement as he watched me out in the barn jump up and down and yell till my throat went dry. How proud he was going to be. I knew what he'd say when he saw me in that uniform, 'Determination will do it for you every time kiddo.'

"The bus stopped at Market Street, but I had another mile to Canton. Those bright yellow socks took off up Main Street past Nottingham's 5 and 10 cent store, Black's clothing store, Thatcher's ice cream parlor; running, running, running—faster and faster—past Kelly's shoeshine parlor, the City Hall, St. Anne's Hospital and finally, Canton Street. I stared at the huge brick building and asked myself, 'Auditorium or gym?' The gym, of course. I threw open the door. Hardly able to breath, I leaned against the wall just inside and slid slowly to the floor. My dangling arms rested on bony knees as my head dropped between them. Without looking up, I watched two familiar, dirty white sneakers with gold shoe laces slowly and hesitantly walk toward me. When the toes of those sneakers kissed the toes of mine, I whispered, 'I didn't make it, did I?' Anne sank to her knees and grabbed my floating hands. Through her tears she answered, 'No. The last uniform was assigned two minutes ago.'

"The silent finality was as deafening as the roar of an angry sea.

"Weeks went by. I sat on a rock wall in a meadow, in a rocking chair on the front porch or under a maple tree changing costume for the fall regalia. There I scribbled all kinds of words and phrases on multiple pieces of paper. Some I kept; most I threw away. But it was during that shifting and tumbling that I discovered the peaceful, rhythmic beauty of words.

"On a brisk fall afternoon, shortly before the school bells rang again, I road my bike out to the stone wall that surrounded my favorite meadow. Sitting on the wall I retrieved a small writing pad from my pocket and read:

My aim had been to jump and cheer
For the team about to punt,
Not from bleachers 'mongst a crowd,
With the leaders down in front.

I'd practiced each and every cheer
In the barn till summer's end,
To make a dream come true at last.
I'd cheer beside a friend.

It finally came, my chance to show
I was the very best,
But fate had other plans that day
And removed me from the test.

A feeling crawled inside my soul.
I didn't know its name.
It asked why I had worked so hard.
It asked who was to blame.

With 'time will heal' friends tried
To soothe.
No consolation there.
Nor could my salty droplets cure
A heart beyond repair.

That heart and I we go in search
Of footprints in the sand
To lead us past the roaring waves,
Hope holding tight our hand.

"Not long after, I found myself walking the halls of Collier High as an exalted senior proud to be Secretary of the class. Anne was Vice President.

"Our football team won the State Championship that year and went to Jacksonville, Florida to play in the eastern seaboard competition. Collier went all the way and won the final game to the familiar cheer, 'Go, team, go' lead by the Collier cheerleaders. Our class President and class Treasurer were star performers out on the field.

"When they came back from Florida, the team and the cheerleaders were greeted by the entire city waving gold and white banners and jumping and singing around a huge bonfire. With pride bursting from every chest, accolades and congratulations were spouted on the steps of the City Hall by the Governor, the Mayor, the Principal of Collier High and the Secretary of the Senior Class.

"On Valentine's Day that year, I received a valentine from a fellow in my chemistry class. I hadn't noticed him before. He was quite handsome and a great basketball player. Smart too. It wasn't long afterward I found myself dancing in a trance to *My Old Flame* at the Y on Saturday nights. We went to the senior prom.

"Oh, and I remained an upstanding member of the Catholic Church."

Emma folds the piece of paper in her lap as Catherine comes over and sits on the railing. She points at Luke with a question mark on her face. Emma just shakes her head and manages a small smile. She gets up and reaches for Catherine's arm. As they walk down the porch she says, "I'm not discouraged, Catherine, really, just a little anxious. I don't have a lot of time."

Catherine looks questioningly at her but says nothing.

I can't seem to ignore her like I can the others. Who's the young girl? Is she the nuisance out there?

That night sleep eludes the exhausted Emma. Her mind refuses to retire; it can't rid itself of two nagging thoughts.

So little time. How am I going to find out if Luke is listening?

Overwhelmed by fear of failure, she tosses and turns.

A wisp of air brushes her forehead. She knows Chocolate has come to comfort her, to let her know there is no need to worry.

Morning finds the sun struggling with a dense fog in its effort to start the day. Emma lies on her side waiting for it to break through the haze. When it doesn't, she gets up and slowly proceeds with her morning routine. After anchoring her French twist with a pearl-studded comb she looks down at her watch and realizes breakfast won't be served for another hour. She sits in her yellow chair by the window and gazes into the heavy mist.

"Where's your faith? After all you're not alone in this endeavor you know. Remember, Himself gave you the job. Oh I know, I know. It's just that I don't want to let Him down and I don't want to let Luke and Margaret down."

Emma smiles as she recalls her father's visit.

"Thanks Chocolate, if my life hadn't been what He needed, He wouldn't have picked me, right?"

On her way to breakfast, she visits the tiny chapel where she finds the sun shining through stained-glass windows.

Like Emma, it has won its struggle.

It's a beautiful day—the kind that calls for climbing mountains and singing out loud. After finishing breakfast, Emma goes out onto the porch and sits down instead of taking her usual morning walk. She closes her eyes and listens to the music of the wind as it flits through millions of leaves clinging to thousands of swaying branches. Footsteps interrupt the symphony as Catherine and Luke walk toward her. Emma continues her peaceful abstraction for a few more minutes then opens her eyes and looks over at Luke.

"Well, how's Luke this morning?"

"You know I'm going to keep asking. Some morning you're going to surprise me and answer."

Oh how I hope that event isn't too far off she pleads silently.

"Let's forget crises for awhile. Okay? Instead, let's move on to decisions.

"High school had ended, and Anne went off to New Rochelle. It was the fall of 1947. I wasn't going anywhere.

"I never wanted to be anything but a nurse, but there wasn't enough money to send me to St. Elizabeth's Hospital in Boston. That's where I was determined to train.

"Not sure what kind of job I could find with four years of Latin and French, I scanned the want-ad section of the newspaper every day. Finally, Dr. Murphy hired me as a dental assistant. Was I thrilled when he told me he'd like me to wear a white uniform and cap.

"However, not much time went by before I realized I was not cut out for dabbling in rich, red blood. I remember, as if it were yesterday, the afternoon I assisted at my first full-mouth extraction. How could I ever forget it? I stood by the dental chair holding a half-moon shaped pan under the patient's chin. It was into my pan Dr. Murphy began to drop, one by one, Mr. Elliot's upper and lower teeth. By the time the fifth tooth plinked onto the bottom of my pan, I was terrified I'd lose my lunch. But it was still making an effort to digest when twenty-two crimson teeth lay abandoned, waiting for me to throw them away.

"In spite of the bumps, I traveled that road for two more years before heeding the detour signs and saying goodbye to Dr. Murphy—my dream of emulating Florence Nightingale cast aside like Mr. Elliot's bloody teeth.

"I asked myself, 'Emma, what now?' I'd never had to ask myself that question before and had no idea in what direction I wanted to go. I did know that whatever I decided to do would require more education than I had. So back to the want ads. It didn't take long to find a job in the cost department of one of the industrial plants in town. How I ever spent eight hours a day, five days a week penning figures into little squares on bright orange cost cards I'll never know. But, after close to a year, I knew if I didn't put down the pen and walk away, I'd soon be escorted through the front door of the state-run funny farm.

"With the money I'd managed to save, plus help from Mama and Daddy and a loan from Aunt Lena and Uncle Emory, I applied to Boston University.

"At the College of Practical Arts and Letters I studied secretarial skills and English literature. By the end of the first year, I could take shorthand at ninety words a minute and type at a hundred and twenty. On top of that, I knew the difference between a debit and a credit. So, I had all the tools I needed and didn't anticipate any trouble finding a well paying position. Executives everywhere needed secretaries.

"Mama urged me to earn at least an Associates Degree, but I didn't want to spend any more of someone else's money or my precious time—some of which had been spent watching angelic brides, their faces obscured by jeweled, beribboned netting, float dreamlike toward their fates, and I remember wondering how such lovely creatures could bury themselves in one place without first exploring the rest of the world.

"The brides were old and dear friends who had no need to watch palm trees sway, climb a peak called Pikes, ride a horse upon the western plains, stride across the Golden Gate Bridge, or, perhaps, shift and tumble words sitting atop a red clay mesa.

"I heard whispers they didn't—whispers telling me to venture beyond safety.

"I listened and pondered,

Life's journey begins
Down a road
Leading where?
At a time when we don't
Even know
That we're here.
It tumbles along,
Like a leaf in the wind,
'Fore it's trapped in the plans
And the plots of earth's men.

Disturbing, the whispers
Invading my soul,
Murmurs that haunt
That persist.
No rest
Till I answer,
Till I query life's course
And start on my journey
O'er mountain and plain,
In search of life's mystery,
Its ultimate aim."

Emma closes her eyes and listens to the symphony of whistling leaves and the wistful rustling of the piece of paper dangling from her fingertips.

Over mountain and plain, In search of life's mystery, Its ultimate aim.

Maybe that's why I listen—the rhythm, the tempo.

Catherine comes out onto the porch to take Luke up to his room for lunch, but Emma doesn't want to let go of the memories, not just yet. Cold chicken sandwiches can wait. Content, she rocks, listens and reminisces until a slight pang of hunger motivates her to get up and go into the dining room. She's also ready for a nice, hot cup of tea.

During lunch she thinks about the story she will begin in the afternoon. She hasn't thought about her days in Hartford, Connecticut for a long, long time. She wonders why. They were some of the best years of her life.

When she finishes her sandwich, Emma beckons to Catherine standing by the sideboard pouring lemonade. Catherine nods her head and goes on serving until she gives the last glass to old Mrs. Henry. Dancing a little jig over to Emma's table she sits down.

"Sure and what can I do for you dear lady?"

"Do you think it would be all right to take Luke for a walk around the porch?"

"I don't see why not. Sure and it's a beautiful day."

Emma hurries off to fetch her shawl and when she returns, finds Luke standing by the front door with Catherine. Linking her arm through his, she begins to walk. No one speaks as they pass the green rockers lined up along the way. Emma nods and stops once or twice to inquire after someone's health, but they stare right through her. She sighs and begins to sing a jaunty little tune that had been popular during her years in Hartford. She had danced many a night away while Doris Day sang *Que Sera Sera.*

Their rockers, quiet and still, have waited patiently. Emma gently sits Luke down and pats his shoulder whispering in his ear, "Yes, Luke, what will be, will be. But we can embellish destiny with the quantity and quality of the world we allow ourselves to experience.

"A long time ago, I made up my mind to allow my life all the adventures it could handle.

"I was twenty-one—that magic age—when I felt the time had come for me to explore the world Shakespeare called a stage where you and I and everyone else are players. I wanted desperately to take part in the performance—not stand by, envious, watching from the wings.

"But I agreed with Mama's advice that perhaps a few rehearsals might be wise before stepping out upon the Bard's boards. And so, I accepted a secretarial position with a local, blustery Pontiac dealer. While he sold Pontiacs, I rehearsed.

"Two years disappeared before a particularly bright morning in April rolled around and changed my life. On that morning I woke up to find sunbeams waltzing on my windowsill. I watched for awhile then got up to join them. Leaning out toward the morning dew, I noticed a red-breasted robin standing on the damp, spring lawn. It seemed to be looking around in rapt anticipation. I watched until it flew away, then suddenly knew I would rehearse no longer.

"For a long time a plan had been biding its time in the recesses of my mind. It came to me one day when I heard the intriguing sound of a distant train whistle as I rode my bicycle along the old country rode up behind my grandmother's, daydreaming of exploring the great big world out beyond my oh, so small one.

"I decided right then and there that when I was ready to leave home, I'd drive down to Collier's train station and buy a ticket for the first city in the United States that came to mind as I walked through the station's door.

"That morning I gave my notice to the burly Mr. Mayo.

"Two weeks later, I walked through the door of Collier's train station, and as I did Hartford, Connecticut popped into my head. I bought a ticket for Hartford, Connecticut.

"At ten o'clock the following morning, I placed my small suitcase on the overhead rack, settled comfortably into the seat below and looked around in rapt anticipation.

"The train's destination was Boston. It was there I waved goodbye to familiar surroundings and transferred to a train bound for Hartford.

"My body rocked with its rhythm as I stared out the window through soot and remnants of sticky fingers. I watched green fields, white church steeples, red-clay earth and blooming, yellow forsythia race by, yet I knew they were standing still. As I stared at this phenomenon I realized I was like the grounded caterpillar blossoming into a graceful butterfly—a butterfly *free* to flit from maple tree to lilac bush to kitchen window sill and then finally to find its way over the pickets of a back-yard fence.

"Reverie eclipsed into reality as the large, steel wheels of the train began to lose their rhythm. I could hardly believe my ears when the conductor strolled down the aisle shouting, 'Haaartfooord.' I smoothed out my tweed blazer and put a comb through my hair which, of late, had become amply sprinkled with tiny white threads. When everyone had left the train, I retrieved my suitcase and climbed down onto the platform. Blinking in the bright sunlight, I shaded my eyes and looked around. I spotted a row of doors and walked briskly toward them, trying very hard to look like I knew where I was going, an extremely difficult task since I had no idea.

"Behind one of the doors, in the middle of an unbelievable amount of space, stood a round, kiosk-type structure with a large sign across the top that read Information. The woman standing behind the counter looked terribly stern. I hesitated before asking for directions to the state employment office. When I did, she just slammed a phone book down on the counter. Did I thank her? I suppose so. I didn't want to.

"I spotted a bench over by the public telephone, and it was then fear, that unseen enemy, invaded my heart.

"I wished I had listened to Mama and reserved a room for the night. I decided to call a hotel before calling the employment agency.

"Hesitantly, I returned to Miss Congeniality of 1953 and asked the name of the principal thoroughfare in Hartford. She bellowed, 'Main Street.' I returned to my bench and found the number for what I hoped would be a satisfactory hotel on Main Street. A room was available, and I began to feel more comfortable.

"I quietly slipped the phone book back on the counter and hurried away in search of a taxi. When it stopped in front of a fine looking hotel, my shoulders slumped down in relief. In as nonchalant a manner as I could manage, I walked toward the front desk and gave my name to the portly, middle-aged gentlemen who had been leering at me as I crossed the elegant lobby. He informed me my room was located on the twelfth floor. A bellboy took the key and escorted me up in the elevator. He unlocked the door and placed my small suitcase just inside—if I hadn't seen it done in the movies, I probably wouldn't have tipped him.

"A huge WOW blanked out every thought as I slowly placed my suitcase on the bed. My eyes wandered toward one of the windows. They blinked twice when I realized the red tiled roof of a building across the street was at eye level. I wanted to go over to the window and look down, but I wasn't quite ready for that.

"Oh, the excitement that burst through me as I continued to look around the room. How grand, grown-up and sophisticated it was. I had often fantasized being in such a room, all by myself, high above the world in a strange, sophisticated city.

"But it had never occurred to me that I'd be lonesome. Love and security had always been built into those castles in the air.

"My elation waned as I sank to the floor. I was alone, on my own. Mama wasn't downstairs. Anxiety slowly crept up on me, then turned to fright, until the silence surrounding me whispered, 'This is the reality of your dreams.' Becoming louder and louder it continued, 'This is why you dabbled in rich, red blood. This is why you penned figures into little squares on orange cost cards and why you went to Boston University. This is why you rehearsed your skills and flew over the back-yard fence with the robin and the butterfly.' I jumped up, whirled around the room and stopped at the window. Cars looked like play toys and people like the captors of Gulliver.

"I unpacked my bag and telephoned the Connecticut State Employment Office. Within a few minutes I had an appointment at nine o'clock the following morning.

"I arrived promptly and was given the necessary shorthand and typing tests. An interview followed with a well groomed, professional looking woman who, strangely enough, reminded me of Mama. She seemed impressed with my qualifications and arranged an interview at two o'clock that afternoon with the Director of Industrial Relations of Maynard Aircraft Corporation. She explained Maynard Aircraft was a company that manufactured helicopters for the Navy and was located a few miles northwest of Hartford. She then supplied me with an appropriate bus schedule, smiled and wished me luck.

"I remember there was a little tearoom across the street, and I had lunch before boarding the one-thirty bus. I asked the driver to let me off at Maynard Aircraft, which he did. I walked through a large parking lot toward the main entrance and was most impressed. I prayed the interview would go well. The receptionist took my name, and I sat down to wait, nervously browsing through a public relations pamphlet. Finally, I heard my name and the receptionist escorted me down the hallway to a Mr. Lapan's office.

"The interview lasted about half an hour, after which I was taken on a tour of the facility. It was fascinating. On the way back to his office, I prayed this man would realize how much he needed me. In my wildest dreams, I had never imagined such a position. When we were again facing each other across his impressive mahogany desk, he smiled and said, 'I'd certainly enjoy saying my new secretary hailed from New Hampshire.' I returned his smile, and replied, 'I'd love having that distinction.' After a brief chat, he escorted me to the front lobby and said he'd look forward to seeing me a week from Monday.

"As I placed my dime in the fare box, the bus driver winked and said, 'Get the job?' I winked back and nodded.

"On the trip back to Hartford, I kept seeing myself sitting at a desk in front of Mr. Lapan's office, an image that continually interrupted my quest for an answer to the gnawing question, 'Where am I going to live?' I had to find at least a room before returning to Collier. Mama's advice to seek help from the nuns, if I found a position and needed a room, pushed through my fantasies and stayed with me till I got back to the hotel. I searched the yellow pages and found listed there a St. Joseph's College in West Hartford.

"The following morning, I knocked on the front door of a white cape with deep green shutters sitting comfortably on a street in West Hartford. Mrs. Hartrandt, a stout, well dressed lady—in the true sense of the word—about seventy years old, answered my knock and invited me in. Within half an hour, I had a sunny, pleasant room where I could hang my hat and a driveway where I could park my car."

Emma rocks in silence.

"Squeak. Squeak. Squeak."

She listens to the soothing sound and, after some thought, decides it's time…she must find out if Luke's mind remains a blank sheet of paper.

This voice and whatever's out there hiding from me are connected somehow. But how? Did I know her before? Before what?

Catherine comes out onto the porch. She notices Emma silently rocking back and forth, Luke sitting still beside her. She's disappointed for she has a few minutes to herself and has been looking forward to the relaxation of listening to Emma's story.

"Sure and it looks like you're done for the afternoon, Emma."

"Yes, Catherine. That's all for today."

"Well then, I guess I'll take Luke for a walk myself. Whadya say Luke me lad, want to take a stroll through the woods?"

"Now there's a good idea, Catherine. The exercise will do you both good,"

Catherine helps Luke up from his chair and puts his arm through hers. She leads him along the porch and down the front steps. Emma watches until they disappear onto a path that circles through the woods.

By the time Catherine's white uniform reappears at the edge of the trees, Emma has worked out a plan.

Catherine returns to the porch after settling Luke in his room. She has sensed Emma wants to talk to her without his being present. She is right.

"Catherine, Margaret is taking Luke home in five more days. I must find out what effect, if any, my stories are having on him. Oh Catherine, I know God chose my life for this job, so why can't I conquer this trepidation?"

Catherine is surprised; she hasn't heard about Margaret's intention to take Luke home. And it certainly isn't like the confident Emma to doubt her ability to make a difference. She can't think of a thing to say. The two women sit quietly side by side, rocking and looking out toward Emma's mighty mountain.

After what seems a terribly long time, Catherine says, "Think about it Emma, Luke was active and talented, enjoyin' a full life, wantin' for nothin'. Then poof, he doesn't even know it existed. What else but another life, ordinary or not, can help him remember there's a world out there beyond his own desolate one? Sure and why shouldn't your life do it Emma? I just know he's listenin'."

"I hope you're right, and I can think of only one way to find out. Return Luke to the back porch—no squeaks, no voices. He mustn't even sense a presence—total solitude. If he's been listening to the stories, it's my hope he'll wonder where I am and get up to look for me. You see Catherine, I'm ninety-nine percent sure I'm the only person he's allowed into his dark and empty existence. But, if he gets up from his chair, I'll need someone to watch from a distance in case he walks directly toward the railing. Or, if he gets up and turns right or left, I'll need someone to guide him in my direction and say, 'Good morning Emma.' Luke will either stop or continue down the porch to nowhere.

"I have no idea what the time factor will be, so I can't ask you to help. I've decided to call Margaret. When I tell her my plan, I'm sure she'll be happy to be the watchdog. What better person to nonchalantly appear and express how pleased she is to see him attempting to walk by himself."

"Sure and it sounds like a good plan to me, Emma. But if you find you do need my help, don't hesitate to holler. Sure and I'd better be gettin' along now though."

Emma gets to her feet and goes in to call Margaret. She is not at home so Emma leaves a message with her answering service. She goes in search of Catherine who's helping out in the dining room.

"Catherine, Margaret wasn't home so I left a message for her to call me back."

About half an hour later, Catherine finds Emma in the chapel and hands her the telephone.

"Oh, Margaret, thank you for returning my call."

Emma explains her plan and returns the phone to Catherine.

"Margaret is going to try to get a room at The Wentworth as soon as she can. This is so important, Catherine"

"Sure and I know that Emma."

Later, as Emma is about to start her dinner, Catherine comes into the dining room and gives her a comforting hug.

"Sure and it's on for tomorrow."

The next morning Emma lies in bed watching the orange horizon disappear into a blue sky. Her thoughts are of Luke, and she wonders what the day will bring.

As she sits up and rests her feet on the little Oriental rug beside her bed, a thought jumps out at her.

"Emma, you idiot, there is no need of worrying about Luke falling over the railing. Oh my, if only my mind at ninety-five could function as well as it did when those numbers were going in the opposite direction."

She rises and prepares herself for this momentous day.

As she steps into the foyer from the elevator, she sees Margaret coming through the front door. She hurries toward her and is thankful for the warm hug.

"Emma, all the way up in the car I've been concerned that I may be too far away to reach Luke if he starts toward the railing."

"Stop worrying, my dear, if Luke isn't on his way back to us, he won't move. If he is, he'll know enough to turn right or left."

Margaret walks along beside Emma as they proceed down the long, back hallway to the rear of the house. The old grandfather clock standing in the foyer is ringing nine o'clock. Margaret's thoughts are of Emma.

She does seem a caring lady. I hope she will not be disappointed. Of course, she could be right; perhaps her stories are bringing Luke back. Could she possibly be more than a sweet, senile old lady? She did ask if I would share her hope. Perhaps I should.

Catherine listens to the comforting sound of the chiming clock as she strolls with Luke along the rear porch toward a waiting rocker. Upon reaching it, she sits Luke down and strokes his head of black curly hair. She turns to see Margaret coming out onto the porch, Emma standing in the doorway. She hurries toward them. Emma smiles her approval, giving them both a thumbs-up before walking back down the long hallway toward the front porch, where she will wait, hope and pray.

"Sure and would you be carin' for a cup of coffee, Mrs. Turnbridge?"

"Yes I would, very much. Thank you, Catherine."

After what seems hours, Catherine returns and Margaret expresses her gratitude with a smile. They both watch the still figure for a few minutes before Catherine winks and hurries off.

Three quarters of an hour slowly creeps by.

What's different? I'm alone. Where is she?

Even though the coffee is now cold, Margaret lifts the cup to her lips. Over the rim she sees Luke making an effort to get out of the chair. She freezes. Luke stands up, teeters back and forth then steadies himself with an arm of the chair. He seems to be trying to decide which way to turn. A few minutes go by before he starts walking down the right side of the porch moving slowly, cautiously, both hands groping the air in front of him. Margaret waits for what she feels is an appropriate amount of time before hurrying toward her son.

"Well Luke here you are. I've been looking for you. Catherine does not seem to be around this morning?"

She takes his arm and continues toward Emma. When they reach her, Margaret says, "Good morning Emma, how are you this beautiful morning?" Emma returns the greeting holding on to her heart. As Margaret starts to proceed, Luke stops and again his hands grope the air until they rest on the back of his rocker. Margaret helps him to sit down. She is so happy she glows as she says, "Did you enjoy the walk, dear?"

All that can be heard is the sound of the boards under Emma's chair.

"Squeak. Squeak. Squeak."

Luke's chair remains still, his blank eyes look out toward Mount Washington; nothing has changed. Margaret's eyes fill with tears while Emma's resemble glittering stars in a black heaven. She winks at Margaret as they talk about the weather and the world in general. After carrying on this banal conversation for a while longer, Emma gets up, and Margaret kisses her son goodbye. The two women walk down the porch in silence. Starting down the front stairs, Margaret turns and looks into Emma's sparkling eyes.

"Why are you so happy? Except for getting up by himself what has been accomplished?"

"Your son is still far away from you and me, but he's listening to my stories. Dear, dear Margaret, he's not a blank page any more. The abyss is not as deep or as black. He has begun his journey. We must both be patient."

Margaret hurries toward her car, not knowing what to think.

Will my eyes ever sparkle like Emma's? She said we must be patient. It is hard to be patient. Oh God, I beg You please return my son.

I know Emma's purpose lies not in Luke's past but motivating him toward a future. But how can she do that with only her life's story? If only I had her faith. Oh, Emma, I beg you also, please bring back my musical miser.

Emma returns to Luke and sits in her rocker trying to control her excitement. She's determined this beautiful morning will be no different than any other—just another day, except it's the day she will begin the story of her life in Hartford, Connecticut.

"So you went for a walk by yourself. Well, good for you. A new experience.

"Luke, did you know that Life keeps her secrets in our experiences, hoping we'll discover them?

"Ah, there's food for a good story –Life's secrets."

Emma is looking forward to telling him about this turning point in her life.

"What wonderful years—those spent in Hartford. So many laughs…so few tears.

"Friends loved to jolly me for having come from New Hampshire. I remember one particular morning. Mr. Lapan had sent me over to the flight hanger with an important piece of correspondence—no faxes in those days. Crossing the hanger's apron, I ran into Al, the chief test pilot. He had to have been one of the handsomest men I have ever seen. He asked if I'd had a nice weekend. I nodded and told him I'd been to New Hampshire. Grinning he replied, 'Emma, when you go home, doesn't your mother find it strange your wearing shoes?' I didn't want to disappoint him, so I pretended to be angry and hurried into the hanger, warmed by the thrill of his attention.

"And then there was Neal—an engineer who worked across the hall from Mr. Lapan's office. Shortly after my encounter with Al, Neal came up behind me in the cafeteria and whispered, 'Emma, do you mind if I pick this piece of straw out of your hair.' I played the game with him too.

"Ah! But one sunny, summer morning, daydreaming as I drove to work along a back-country road, I suddenly had to slam on the brakes. One of the local farmers was lackadaisically prodding his brown and white cows across the road toward a pasture filled with golden buttercups playing in the sunshine. I waited patiently, all the while enjoying my thoughts of sweet revenge. Fifteen minutes later, I arrived just in time to see Mr. Lapan come out of his office wearing a rather quizzical expression as he stared at my empty chair. I walked up to him, wearing the sweetest smile I could muster, and said, 'Of all the years I worked in New Hampshire, I was never late because I had to wait for the cows to cross the road.' Without a word, he turned and went into his office.

"News of my retaliation spread, and the kidding slowly went away.

"Time hurried along while friends and I shared life's experiences—each friend special for a different reason. Maggie, a nurse, had bright blue eyes that never stopped sparkling. Peg, a secretary, had a smile that devastated every male at Maynard. And then there was Lois, the oh, so smart one.

"Many, many a weekend Maggie, Peg and I skied till the sun went down right here in these very mountains. Lois would rather read.

"I was comparatively content with my life in Hartford but must admit I wondered now and then what lay beyond. I continued my daydreaming about actually seeing the whole world.

"I remember one particularly beautiful Saturday morning in July. I packed myself a light lunch and drove down by the Connecticut shore where I found a lonely stretch of beach away from the crowds and protected by a high, rocky bluff. It seemed to be waiting just for me. I dropped down on the sand and delighted in the wind's fingers rumpling my hair and the sun's smile warming my bony shoulders. I stared out over the broad blue expanse toward a distant horizon. The salty smell of the sea and the pounding sound of the surf enhanced the mystery that lay beyond its limits.

"Blindly, I watched the waves creep toward my buried toes then retreat as if afraid to go further. Repetition enhanced their courage, and the dampened sand boldly receded beneath my feet. I looked up and smiled as two yelling yellow sailboats skipped along the horizon like two playful children enjoying a game of tag.

"When they were out of sight, I retreated from the advancing tide. On dry sand again, I retrieved my writing pad from the picnic basket lying beside me. Absentmindedly, I began to tumble and shift words, listening and hoping to hear a cadence of the sea's ancient wisdom. I sat, wrote and eavesdropped. All the while the waves rolled in and the waves rolled out. I was still there when the sun gave up and went home. When the blue of the sea turned black and all I could hear was its roar, I gave up too.

"Later that night, propped against the bed pillows, I leaned over and picked up my writing pad. Flipping back the cover, I scanned the labors of my meditative day.

I sit upon the cool, wet sand
Of this the eastern shore,
Watching a rolling surf creep near,
Tickle my toes then disappear.
And I wonder,
If I sat upon the cool, wet sand
Of a distant western shore,
Would the sea come close
To play with me?
I smile, of course it would.

Whether here of there
The sea's the sea
Of tides and surf
Flowing wild and free.
I listen for its wisdom
Hidden way down deep from me,
Till 'cross the lace-edged waves
I hear a breath upon the air,
'Like me, just be,
What matter where?'

"I shut off the light and wondered in the darkness, am I where I'm going or am I where I've been? Questions I'd asked myself before.

"The sea had shared a secret. 'What matter where?' Did it warn me to heed the constant rhythms of my shifting tides?

"I wasn't sure and remained in Hartford."

"Churlee. Churlee. Churlee."

The purple finch warbles its familiar song.

Catherine comes out onto the porch to announce lunch is served. Emma gets up and walks as far as the dining room with Catherine and Luke who continue on toward the elevator.

She hears a breath upon the air. That's cool, but it's no breath I want to hear.

After lunch, as Catherine settles Luke in his chair, Emma is almost sure she detects an aura of anticipation coming from his still figure. Perhaps it's only her imagination, but what matter. He's listening. She smiles at Catherine who's decided to steal a few minutes and hops up onto the porch railing. Her wink bolsters Emma's confidence.

"Hi Catherine, glad you could join us.

"I was about to tell Luke that as I listened to the wind whisper and whistle through the trees last night, I seemed to hear the inspiring words of Bruce Barton being repeated over and over, like an echo, 'Nothing splendid has ever been achieved except by those who dared believe that something inside them was superior to circumstance.'

"Mr. Barton, you know, was a man much more impressed by Christ's exceptional ability to lead than by His divinity.

"I never let go of his wisdom throughout a harrowing experience that began on a bright, sunny day in late October, 1954 at Maynard Aircraft.

"On that day, during its maiden flight, the S-31 helicopter crashed shortly after takeoff.

"Tears flowed, it seemed, forever.

"Al, Maynard's chief test pilot…remember? The one who liked to kid me because I came from New Hampshire, hung onto life in a Hartford hospital while family, friends and co-workers attended the funeral of his co-pilot and closest friend. Al and Charlie had grown up together, flying newspaper airplanes over a shared, backyard fence.

"Except for his immediate family, Al was not allowed visitors at Hartford Hospital. Nevertheless, his Maynard family reached him with mountains of cards and notes and waited patiently to touch his hand, pat his shoulder or kiss his cheek. As it turned out, we had to be very, very, very patient.

"Many weeks went by before Al recovered enough to return to his home in Simsbury—a small town about fifteen miles north of West Hartford on the other side of Simsbury Mountain. A beautiful ride on any spring, summer or fall day but not on a windy, rainy, winter night.

"Trips to Simsbury were scheduled by the Personnel Department to avoid Al being bombarded by too many well meaning visitors. Everyone had to wait his or her turn. Lois and I were slated for the same day and had to wait four weeks before it finally arrived.

"As I drove to work that morning, a blustery wind rocked the car. Cold drizzle clouded the windshield—drizzle that would turn to pelting rain by noon. As the day crept toward five o'clock, a heavy mist replaced the rain and turned Maynard's parking lot into an eerie, gloomy place. Cars sat hidden. Lights, enshrouded by ghosts, swayed in the gusty wind. A thin layer of ice covered the pavement, threatening all who ventured forth. Lois and I stood in the swirling fog and pondered the advisability of driving over Simsbury Mountain on such a night. Since we'd waited so long for our chance to see Al, we decided to give it a try. Lois would pick me up at 6 o'clock.

"I had moved from my room at Mrs. Hartrandt's to a larger one, with its own bath, on the third floor of a stately English Tudor-style home in an area of West Hartford closer to Maynard

Aircraft. The house sat high on a steep knoll, all but invisible among noble evergreens and sprawling maples—an imposing structure, mysterious in a way, not the eeriness of Edgar Allen Poe, more the cloudy intrigue of Charlotte and Emily Bronte."

Reflecting for a moment, Emma adds, "Oh, I'm sorry, Luke, you probably aren't familiar with Poe or the Brontes. They were popular authors even before my time."

"Anyway, Mrs. Beckerley, my new landlady, possessed a soft manner and caring heart. She reminded me of Mrs. Fairfax, the housekeeper Charlotte Bronte placed in Mr. Rochester's Thornfield in her book *Jane Eyre.* However, unlike Mrs. Fairfax, Mrs. Beckerley had two memorable idiosyncrasies. She wore bright…and I mean…*bright* red polish on the nails of her long, pencil-thin fingers and she firmly believed that spirits, bereft of their own humanity, roamed the world watching us struggle with ours. She also believed they intervened once in awhile.

"She often invited me to join her for a cup of tea when I came in from work. She loved to tell me stories from the past. Especially those times she'd seen graceful ghosts coming or going through closed doors or departing the bodies of friends and relatives. I would listen with feigned awe, but must admit I experienced a shiver now and then.

"On this particular evening, as I ran up the stairs, I heard a soft, weak voice call my name. I stopped and went into Mrs. Beckerley's bedroom and found her sitting on the edge of the bed. She told me her stomach had been upset all afternoon. I asked if she would like a cup of boiling water, which I felt might help to settle her stomach. She nodded. I went downstairs to put the kettle on. While waiting for the water to boil, I placed a lace doily and a china cup and saucer, cheery with dancing violets, on her favorite mahogany tray. As a final touch, I added a delicately embroidered lavender napkin. The kettle whistled. I filled the cup and returned to the second floor.

"Placing the tray on her bedside table, I asked if there was anything else I could do for her. She shook her head and wearily reached for the pretty china cup. I left her there and raced up to the third floor where I quickly changed into my favorite skirt made of yards and yards of brown tweed wool. Later, I'd wish I hadn't.

"A horn blared and I hurried downstairs. Half way to the first floor I stopped and ran back to make sure Mrs. Beckerley was all right. She was still sitting on the edge of her bed sipping the hot water. She waved me away, saying, 'Don't worry, I'll be fine. The warmth of the water seems to help. Thank you. Be careful, it's a bad night.' In my haste, I failed to notice just how weak her voice had been.

"I grabbed my raincoat from the clothes tree in the front foyer and carefully made my way down the long, steep driveway to Lois' car. As we journeyed over Simsbury Mountain, the road conditions took a back seat to our anticipation of seeing Al. We arrived safe and sound, only to find we weren't expected on such a wild and stormy night. Al's look of surprise quietly transformed into a warm smile of appreciation. We gave him hugs, and he squeezed our hands.

"Lois and I shared the latest Maynard news and gossip. We absorbed the warmth that had nothing to do with roaring flames dancing in the ancient brick fireplace. We forgot the dripping drizzle and roaring wind until Al's wife reminded us the storm was becoming more unfriendly by the minute. Lois and I looked out the window and remembered Simsbury Mountain. We left with loving hugs and regret.

"We hadn't traveled very far when we realized we were in trouble. Cars were sliding, skidding and crashing into each other and into guardrails. Lois inched along, climbing slowly up the treacherous mountain. Her eyes never left the road; the knuckles of her hands seemed about to burst through her skin. I held my breath as I stretched my legs and pressed my feet into the floorboards. I watched blinding headlights come sliding toward us—positive the next one wouldn't miss. We finally stopped climbing; Lois parked by the side of the road, and we sat staring into an opaque world. Our heads turned; our eyes met. We had both realized our descent would be as hazardous, if not more so. Lois smiled halfheartedly and assured me all would be fine if we just took it easy. How mistaken she was.

"Half way down the mountain, the car started to slide. It spun around once, twice before crashing into a guardrail. Lois' hands flew to her face. Blood gushed through her fingers onto the steering wheel and splattered on the dashboard. She grabbed the kerchief from her head and held it up to her face. I gaped in horror. Then I felt it—an excruciating pain shooting up my right arm which had been slammed against the dashboard. But we were both lucky. Lois had only split her bottom lip, and my arm, though painful, was not broken. We got out of the car to find its right front fender had been pushed against the tire. Lois got back into the car and attempted to back it off the guardrail. But it wouldn't move.

"We took turns standing in the wind and the rain hoping someone would stop to help us.

"After what seemed hours, two men appeared out of nowhere and pulled the fender out far enough to enable Lois to back up onto the road. We thanked our deliverers profusely and bombarded heaven as Lois cautiously continued down the mountain. Thank goodness sympathetic saints were listening.

"Lois dropped me off at the end of Mrs. Beckerley's driveway about two o'clock and continued on alone to Windsor Locks.

"My arm throbbed as I tried, unsuccessfully, to climb the steep, icy driveway. It might as well have been Mt. Everest. I finally had to get down on my hands and knees. To this day I have no idea how I ever reached the front door, but I will never forget how I felt when I finally collapsed against it, so thankful to be home and safe. My warm bed was waiting. All I had to do was climb three flights of stairs."

"This is getting too interesting Emma. Sure and I'd better get back to work. See you two later."

Emma smiles at Catherine and continues.

"Holding onto my arm, I slowly climbed to the second floor. My foot felt so heavy as I was about to take that first step up to the third floor. But I never took it. There was a light coming from Mrs. Beckerley's room and the door had been left wide open. This was very unusual. She always closed her door before retiring. I tiptoed across the hall and, feeling quite guilty, peeked into the room. Mrs. Beckerley was where I had left her. But she had fallen back onto the bed. Her arms seemed stiff and her long, thin fingers appeared to be grabbing the side of the mattress. My eyes became fixed on her scarlet fingernails, for some reason brighter than ever. Had she fallen asleep? I crept toward the bed. Mustering all my courage, I placed my hand on her cold, gray one and whispered, 'Mrs. Beckerley.' She didn't answer. She didn't move. I shivered for she never would.

"Overwhelmed with fright, I stood petrified by the bed. I couldn't stop shaking. I just stood there and stared. Finally, I realized I had to do something—call someone. There was an address book on the bedside table next to the tray I had placed there earlier. I shivered again. Picking up the little book, I flipped through it and found the name of a Dr. Adams. In spite of the hour, I knew I had to call. I dialed, hardly able to breathe, and listened as the phone rang and rang. At last an unhappy voice answered. Distraught, I tried to explain what had happened and asked what I should do. In a now angry voice, Dr. Adams replied he hadn't seen Mrs. Beckerley in over two years and hung up. Panic-stricken, I ran out of the room, down the stairs and stood numb in the foyer—my arm forgotten. If it had fallen off, I wouldn't have noticed.

"I have no idea how long I stood there before focusing on the table standing against the wall under the stairs. I shook away the cobwebs that had invaded my brain and blinked at the telephone sitting there on top of a telephone book. I walked toward it. Slowly I reached for the directory and looked up the number of the West Hartford Police Department, then dialed. That was my first mistake.

"A gruff, masculine voice answered, 'West Hartford PD.' I hesitated, then told a perfect stranger the most traumatic experience of my life. Without comment, he asked where I was.

In a cold, dispassionate voice he informed me someone would be right along. The dial tone whirred in my ear.

"I went into the sunroom, still numb and quite frightened, to sit and wait.

"As the shock wore off and reality set in, I heard wind howling and icy rain crash against the windows. My arm began to throb. I wondered about Lois. I thought about Mrs. Beckerley upstairs and looked around the room where we had had so many interesting and eerie conversations.

"There on the table under the front windows sat the drawstring purse she'd had made from an old tapestry that once belonged to her mother. I felt a tear wet my cheek. She would no longer remove change from her wallet and place it in the purse—a ritual performed every time she came home. When the purse was full, she would take the coins to the bank.

"Could it only be a few hours since she'd waved me away?

"I knew my landlady's spirit lingered.

"Her eighteenth-century desk seemed to be staring at me. I wondered about an envelope I knew was in there tucked away somewhere—an envelope containing two thousand dollars. It belonged to a friend of her late husband who had visited about two weeks ago. She had told me about it just the day before.

"Burrr—Burrr—Burrr."

"I stiffened…frightened. How long had the doorbell been ringing? I got up and hurried to the front door. When I opened it, two tall, husky men in blue uniforms stood staring at me. A cold and insensitive voice asked if I was the one who had called about a dead landlady. I could only nod my head. The cold, callous voice wanted to know where she was. I pointed toward the stairway. And in unison they said, 'Lead the way.' I hesitated, preferring to remain downstairs. Without a word, they each roughly grabbed an arm and lifted me to the top of the stairs. Horrified, I pointed to Mrs. Beckerley's room. They left me agape in the hallway and disappeared.

"It must have been a year later when they came out of the bedroom and asked if I'd called anyone else. I told them about my conversation with Dr. Adams. In the same bullying manner, they escorted me into the bedroom. I noticed the room had been roughly searched. Mrs. Beckerley would have been so hurt at such an intrusion.

"When I looked down and saw a highly polished black boot crushing a dainty, lavender napkin, I could no longer contain my tears. A raging river flowed down my cheeks."

Emma stops to reflect for just a moment. She doesn't notice the sun disappearing behind an ominous, black cloud. Thunder roaring in the distance catches her attention.

What's she gonna do now?

Catherine and Marie come running.

"Come on Luke. We better get you inside. Sure and it won't be long 'fore that rain starts comin' down."

Marie helps Emma up from her chair and takes her arm.

"I'm fine, Marie, go and take care of the chairs. Go along now. Really, I'm perfectly capable of getting inside by myself."

Marie pushes the rockers as close to the house as she can.

Sitting up in her room by the window, Emma surrenders to sorrow as she contemplates Mrs. Beckerley's final hours. She's never forgiven herself for leaving her alone on that stormy night so long ago.

As she stares off into the distance through the rain, another, more pleasant memory transports her to the shores of the St. Lawrence River on its journey from Lake Ontario to the Atlantic Ocean. It was the first week of July back in 1955.

She sees Edgewood Resort perched upon the shore of one of the river's thousand islands. Lois' friends Jum and George are smiling from the steps of the wide front porch, their arms outstretched, anxious to begin their hospitality. They had left Hartford years before to escape the hustle and bustle of a city grown too large.

When they found Edgewood, it was long past its heyday—the buildings dilapidated, the landscape overgrown and the color of sun-burned wheat. Jum and George bought the property anyway for they intended to reintroduce early nineteenth century grandeur to the vacationing public. They worked long laborious hours to restore the buildings and what had been resplendent grounds to their former glory. But they soon realized it would be far too costly an endeavor. They also had forgotten to take into consideration the income tax—a tax that had put an end to the kind of wealth a vacationing public would need to enjoy the magnificence of bygone years. And so they changed their plans. Edgewood became famous for, among other things, its western frontier town. Twice a day, banks were robbed, bandits jailed and rustlers hanged from tree limbs.

Emma and Lois spent their summer vacations at Edgewood. They swam, skied behind a speeding motor boat, relaxed dripping wet on a sun-drenched wharf and dined and danced on a moonlit terrace where background music enhanced a young girl's dream of romance.

With Mrs. Beckerly now tucked away in the recesses of her mind, Emma watches the rain and speaks to the memory of a handsome young man she once thought she loved.

"It was a beautiful evening. I can almost hear the music that shared the night with our laughter as Lois and I dined on the moon-drenched terrace—so romantic under those trillions of stars sparkling on the river ambling far below.

"I didn't see you cross the terrace, Sim. I didn't even know you existed until your hand pressed my shoulder and I looked up into the bluest eyes I'd ever seen—even bluer than Maggie's or Mama's. Your blond, wavy hair, obviously not combed in quite awhile, topped a smile that melted my heart. You asked me to dance.

"I knew I would never, ever be the same again. Life, as I knew it, disappeared into the night.

"My feet never touched the ground for the rest of the week. I was your girl. How I loved being the envy of every female on the dock. Imagine me being able to hold the attention of Edgewood's handsome and popular Recreational Director.

"I never even considered learning to water ski, but you insisted I at least try. How patient you were. But you never did convince me to go off that six-foot jump you rigged in front of the main dock. I just couldn't do it. But how everyone loved to watch *you* sail through the air off that jump. The guests would rather watch you than ski themselves or go for a ride in the speedboat.

"I cringe when I think of the times you skied off that jump backwards. The guests—even Jum and George—held their breaths as the speedboat swerved inches from the side of the jump and you spun around skiing in reverse up the wet planks before bursting like a Greek god into the atmosphere. Oh the sighs of relief when you descended, beautifully balanced, onto the water. How you laughed as you bowed and waved.

"It's too bad you had to work all the time. But I must admit I loved leisurely gliding through the water on midnight cruises to one island or another for picnics in the moonlight. I remember the music seemed to be mysteriously floating toward the boat from islands silhouetted against the dark horizon. How you managed that I never knew.

"But I do know I helped you create an aura of romance.

"Remember the Fourth? What a shame it had to rain. There wasn't much for the guests to do except play cards, read or catch up on postcards. Who expected rain? It hadn't been forecast. But Jum expected you to come up with something to keep the guests entertained didn't he? And you asked me to help put on a water-skiing exhibition. Where did I ever find the courage? Must have been from the depths of love; it certainly wasn't confidence in my skiing ability.

"We had so much fun. And it must have been contagious because the guests seemed to be having even more fun as they watched from the gazebo and the front porch. Time flew by—the rain forgotten.

"Will I ever forget the finale? You wanted me to sit on your shoulders. I admit I had to think about that one. But with a little coaxing I agreed. You swung me up and I tucked my legs tightly around your back. The boat sped over the water. We crossed back and forth across its wake and I remember I just sparkled with delight.

"I guess you sensed a need for diversity when you yelled at me to stand up. I don't know why, or how, but I didn't hesitate, just swung my feet up onto your shoulders and lifted my arms in the air. Why I didn't kill myself I'll never know.

"I can still hear the clapping and hollering reaching us through the rain.

"Oh, but you were a devil—a devil right out of the pits. Before I knew what was happening, the boat swerved and headed for the jump. You skied up the wooden planks and I screamed 'Noooooo' as I flew into the air and disappeared below the waves. My head popped out of the water as the boat circled back. It was a miracle I didn't collide with the floating skis. Oh, but how wonderful your arms felt when you leaned over and scooped me up onto your hip. We skied to the dock, you holding the rope with one hand and me with the other. How we laughed.

"Around midnight, we sat on the dock for a long time listening to the dark water invisibly vital under a shrouded moon. You took my hand and told me what a great sport you thought I was. I smiled and you stood up pulling me with you. The mist had disappeared into drifting clouds, and the moon winked. Oh yes, the moon winks. It knew something had happened between you and me as we stood silent, our eyes revealing what lay deep in our hearts. You reached out for me and wound your arms tightly around me. Why did I have to cry when you kissed me? I tried not to, but I always do, don't I, when I'm overwhelmed by emotion. We held each other gently. Then you looked down at me and smiled that wonderful smile that always melted my heart. As if in a dream, we walked down the dock away from the river shining now in the moonlight—a river that had helped make our moment so special.

"But joy doesn't last very long, does it? The next day she arrived—your mother. You hadn't told me she was coming and didn't introduce me to her. In fact, I didn't see you all day. It wasn't till after dinner, as the sun dropped off behind the horizon, that I noticed you and your mother sitting in the gazebo down by the water's edge. You didn't seem to be talking—just looking out over the water. I remember not liking what I felt.

"Later that evening I watched her drive away. You had disappeared. The next day you were busier than a one-armed paperhanger. I spotted you going into the bar just before dinner and hurried to catch up. When I asked if I'd be seeing you later, you said you were going into town with the guys.

"Somehow I couldn't share any of this with Lois.

"I packed most of the day on Friday. At dinner Lois wanted to know why I had spent the day packing when we weren't leaving till Sunday. I shared my anguish. She sympathized, and we planned to leave the next day directly after breakfast.

"But we didn't know George and Jum had planned a huge farewell party for Saturday night. They were so sweet. We couldn't disappoint them after learning they were in the midst of creating an Ezio-Pinza *enchanted evening* for us. And so we stayed till Sunday.

"When we sauntered into the bar about six o'clock, everyone shouted, 'Surprise.' I searched the crowd for you, but you weren't there. Your friend Mike whispered in my ear that you were suffering from the flu. I sat on a barstool and tried to ignore the ache in my heart. I laughed and chatted with everyone around me. I tried to be part of the gaiety. I tried to contribute to the fun. Only Lois knew the supreme effort I was making.

"Jum announced lobster and shrimp were being served on the terrace—my favorite place, my favorite foods. I tried to eat, but tears burning behind my eyelids made it very difficult. They escaped when everyone agreed the last piece of chocolate cake should be saved for you. I blamed Mike for my tears. I said he'd blown smoke in my eyes.

"Dear Jum, you wouldn't allow the dancing to begin until Lois and I promised we'd return Labor Day weekend for the huge celebration being planned for summer's end."

Emma's memories are interrupted by the angry rain pounding louder and louder upon her window.

"Well now, I didn't mean to get so wrapped up in that part of my past. I hope I haven't missed dinner."

She looks down at her watch and pushes herself out of the chair.

"I'm pretty sure I heard Catherine say we're having apple pie tonight. Hope it's topped with whipped cream."

Emma slowly saunters down the hall to the elevator wondering whatever became of Sim.

The next morning Emma wakens early. She doesn't tarry in bed this morning, but gets up to see what's going on beyond her window. Leaning on the windowsill, she watches the sun glistening on rain-soaked trees.

What fun when stars twinkle in the daytime.

I find it so intriguing that no one spot ever remains the same for very long. How imaginative He is. I'm really looking forward to making His acquaintance.

He's given the sky this morning that shade of blue He gives to roaring waves just before they break and splash upon the unsuspecting sand. Yet this afternoon, that same sky may be reminiscent of a climbing, blue morning-glory.

Yesterday the trees swayed like ballerinas; today they dance as if on a Broadway stage. Tomorrow we may have a performance of ragtime.

Emma waves to her small, enchanting world and goes to prepare for the upcoming day.

Downstairs she finds Catherine helping Marie serve breakfast and inquires about Matthew and Pat.

"Oh the lads are fine, Emma, and, as usual, not payin' much attention to me. I've accepted Pat's decision, but can't quite come to grips with Matthew's.

"Oh, oh, sure and it's Mrs. Henry beckonin'. Talk to you later."

Emma finishes her coffee and walks out onto the porch where she finds Luke silent and still.

She sits down and listens to the sound of the floor boards for just a minute, then continues her story.

"Well, Luke, shall we go on with the story of Mrs. Beckerley?

"My flood of tears made no impression on those two police officers.

"One of them asked where they might find the name of Mrs. Beckerley's doctor. I tried to regain some composure and told him probably in her desk downstairs in the sunroom, but that it was most likely locked. He left. As I turned to follow, the other officer asked what I had put in the water. My heart stopped and my tongue refused to function. I just stared at him. Again he asked, "What did you put in the water?" My fog of fear began to lift. I looked at him, not defiantly but with assurance, and informed him I had put nothing in the water. I then suggested he have the cup and its contents analyzed. His eyes reflected the menace in his voice when he said he didn't think that would be necessary since I'd probably already emptied the cup and refilled it.

"Stunned I said no more but was incredulous to think he could possibly suspect I had poisoned Mrs. Beckerley. Fear again fell across my soul while self-preservation warned me to pay attention.

"Without another word, he gestured toward the door. I led him downstairs into the foyer where he went to the telephone and called for an ambulance. When he hung up, he followed me into the sunroom. His partner was surveying Mrs. Beckerley's desk. It was locked. They began to pry it open. I sat down in the chair by the window and wondered if they should be doing what they were doing without a search warrant. However, I was not about to ask any questions.

"I wondered if I should tell them about the envelope containing two thousand dollars. I shivered—it wasn't cold. My arm began to throb and I battled threatening tears. A noise interrupted my thoughts. The desk had snapped open. Rough hands threw about Mrs. Beckerley's neatly organized papers and beloved treasures. One of the officers held up a small, red leather address book. Thumbing through it, he walked into the foyer. When he came back, he told his partner Mrs. Beckerley's physician was on his way.

"While we waited for the doctor and ambulance to arrive, their cold, impudent questions continued. What was my name? How long had I lived there? Where did I work? How did I spend my spare time? On and on. I tried to tell them about the accident and the pain in my arm, but they weren't interested. When I blurted out, 'There's a large sum of money hidden somewhere in that desk,' they were interested.

"I explained that just the day before Mrs. Beckerley had informed me a friend of her late husband had visited from New York City and he had given her two thousand dollars to hold for him. She wanted me to know that she had placed it in an envelope and put it in her desk. I told the officers that I had strongly suggested she deposit the money in a bank, but she insisted the gentleman had specifically requested she not do so. They went back to the desk and resumed scattering papers, but there was no sign of the envelope.

"The doorbell rang. I jumped out of my chair, startled and frightened. It sounded to me like a gong opening the inner sanctum of a Chinese torture chamber. A strong, brutal hand pushed me back into the chair. Its owner stood over me while his partner went into the foyer. Dr. Beechum had arrived. I couldn't hear what was being said, but I watched as he and my two tormentors climbed the stairs. When they returned to the sunroom, Dr. Beechum came over to me. He smiled and put his hand on my shoulder before taking a seat at the other end of the room.

"We all sat in silence waiting for the ambulance.

"Funny, I never once thought about how they had all managed to get up the driveway.

"The ringing of the phone caused me to jump again. I was given a warning glance as the other officer went into the foyer. He returned and told us the ambulance had been in an accident. But another would be on its way as soon as one was available.

"Dr. Beechum pointed out there was no way the ambulance would ever make it up the driveway. He'd had to park on the street and crawl up on his hands and knees. He asked the policemen how they'd managed. 'Chains.' the grumpier of the two answered, then added he'd better call the ambulance service and tell them to have the driver bring sand and a shovel.

"The officer standing by the table next to my chair picked up Mrs. Beckerley's drawstring purse and asked me what it was. I explained Mrs. Beckerley's daily ritual. Without warning, he emptied its contents into my lap, weighing down the yards and yards of material in my brown wool skirt. 'Count it.' he said. Dr. Beechum sprang from his chair and said in a very angry voice, 'I don't think that's necessary.' The reply, 'You take care of your job, doc, and I'll take care of mine.' sent the good doctor back to the other end of the room. I counted the coins, my hands trembling, my arm aching, my heart pounding. When

I finished, stacks of coins—thirty-four dollars and seventeen cents worth—were piled on the table. The officer recorded the amount in an official looking black book. The coins were dumped back into the purse.

"The front doorbell rang again. I made no attempt to move. Dr. Beechum and I waited without a word as the more civil of the two officers opened the front door. Two ambulance attendants, one carrying a large aluminum stretcher, stepped into the foyer. It seemed hours before we heard the sounds of Mrs. Beckerley's body being maneuvered down the stairs. Dr. Beechum came over and put his arm around my shoulders before escorting me to the other end of the room. His thoughtfulness spared me the trauma of seeing her body removed. I thanked this kind man but didn't share with him I was quite sure Mrs. Beckerley's spirit would be lingering for awhile.

"For the first time since I'd arrived home, I heard Mrs. Beckerley's grandfather clock chime softly over in the corner of the foyer where it always stood waiting patiently for its time to sing. I couldn't believe I hadn't heard it before. I truly loved the old timepiece and had always listened for its comforting sound. It chimed five times.

"Before he left, Dr. Beechum gave me two pills, one for the pain in my arm and one to help me sleep. The officers gave me a warning not to leave the house.

"I closed the front door and collapsed against it, as I'd done earlier—but on the other side eons and eons ago.

"Without knowing how or when, I found myself on the third floor. I went into the bathroom and took the two pills. As time went on, it became apparent the doctor had mistakenly given me pills made of sugar.

"I paced back and forth, back and forth, time forgotten until I noticed light seeping through the trees. I sat down on the antique chair Mrs. Beckerley had put in my room after she'd found out how much I'd admired it. How thoughtful she'd always been.

"I stared into space and wondered where her spirit waited.

"A noise shook me from my contemplation, and I bolted from the chair."

Emma looks up at Catherine who has been sitting on the railing listening.

"My throat feels awfully dry Catherine. Would you mind getting me a cup of tea? Perhaps Luke would like a coke."

She couldn't kill anyone.

Catherine returns with the tea and the coke. She reminds Emma it's almost time for lunch. Emma nods, rocks and enjoys her tea.

"We'll continue after lunch, Luke."

Later, her salad eaten, Emma watches from the dining room window as Catherine brings Luke back out to his chair. She stares at the young man sitting so still.

Is he waiting for me?

She sighs, gets up and joins him out on the porch.

"Well Luke, the noise I'd heard was the front door bell. I let it ring; I didn't have the energy to climb down three flights of stairs.

"'Honk! Honk! Honk!' penetrated my exhaustion, and I looked out the window. They were back. I rushed down the three flights of stairs to open the front door. My two 'friends' were not happy and wanted to know why I hadn't answered the doorbell. I lied and told them I couldn't hear it up on the third floor. I invited them to go up and listen for themselves. They shook their heads and wanted to know why all the lights were on. I explained I'd been frightened when everyone left. I didn't tell them Mrs. Beckerley's spirit lingered somewhere in the shadows.

"They checked all the rooms on the first floor. I wondered if they thought I'd stolen the silver and decided if they thought I'd murder her, I guess they'd think I'd steal from her.

"The grandfather clock struck seven. The officers seemed satisfied everything was in order. Before departing, they warned me not to leave town. I reminded them I worked at Maynard Aircraft. They nodded and were gone.

"Their intrusion had snapped me back to reality, and I went into the kitchen to make myself a cup of coffee. After a shower and change of clothes, I felt better and could think more clearly. My arm ached but definitely felt better; my fright had waned. But my anger was beginning to demand attention.

"A few minutes later, I opened the front door to leave…then hesitated. I couldn't leave without saying goodbye. I closed the door and stood in the foyer a few seconds, sort of looking around. Then silently told Mrs. Beckerley that I'd be back when I was allowed. I also told her I was sorry for being afraid of her and that I knew she stayed to protect me not to harm me. Aloud I said, 'Goodbye for now.'

"I left and carefully backed down the steep driveway—thankful for the sand left behind by the ambulance driver—and drove to Maynard Aircraft. The roads were still slippery, though the wind and rain had ceased. When I arrived, I immediately went to Maggie's office. She listened to my story but didn't ask any questions. She just gave me a hug and told me not to move. She returned shortly with a sedative she'd obtained from Dr. Bagnall and led me out to her car. She brought me home to her mother. Miraculously, in just a few seconds a nightgown had been slipped over my head and a sheet tucked under my chin. I often wonder if I responded to the comforting smile on the face of my friend.

"The next morning I was totally disoriented as I wandered into Mrs. Krickchen's kitchen. The familiar aroma of coffee helped me to focus. Slowly, the image of Mrs. Beckerley's stiff, cold body emerged from my confusion. I wept and drank the coffee. Without a word, Mrs. Krickchen served me scrambled eggs and toast. When I finished eating, she told me to call Mr. Lapan.

"Mr. Lapan's voice expressed a great deal of concern. He informed me a Mr. Kingford, Mrs. Beckerley's lawyer, had called several times requesting I get in touch with him as soon as possible. I did so immediately. Mr. Kingford had a soft, quiet voice and seemed a kind man. I prayed he would be.

"He wanted to tell me that Dr. Beechum had called to say he was ninety-nine percent sure Mrs. Beckerley had died of a heart attack. But he added that the West Hartford Police Department had requested an autopsy. I knew why but kept it to myself for now. When I hung up, I called Maggie and asked if she could pick me up.

"On the way to Maynard Aircraft, I implored her to pray that Mrs. Beckerley hadn't left me any money and to pray even harder that she hadn't initiated her own journey into the spirit world. Maggie's blue eyes widened as she turned to stare at me. My green eyes—widened even more—stared right back. Maggie realized then that if Mrs. Beckerley had done either or both, I was in big trouble.

"I shared with her my earlier conversation with Mr. Kingford. We both agreed all I could do now was wait for the completion of the autopsy and the reading of Mrs. Beckerley's will.

"Mr. Lapan offered me the services of his lawyer if and when I needed them.

"I didn't at the time but was thankful to know they were available if I did. What I needed was an apartment. As it happened, I was very fortunate and found a convenient, three-room apartment in Windsor, a small town south of Maynard Aircraft.

"Time crawled by as if trying to delay impending doom.

"Within a few days, Mr. Kingford called with the results of the autopsy. Mrs. Beckerley had died of a heart attack...nothing else. I had not been named in her will.

"My sigh of relief must have been deafening.

"I expected Mr. Kingford to say goodbye, but he went on to tell me we still had a problem. The two thousand dollars was still missing along with Mrs. Beckerley's three-carat diamond ring. Everything else had been accounted for. I asked if the police thought I had them. He was silent. Before he could answer, I asked if *he* thought I had them. He calmly answered yes to the first question and no to the second. I was silent. He then told me Second Lieutenant Murphy of the Investigative Unit of the West Hartford Police Department would be expecting us at two o'clock the following afternoon. He asked me to meet him in the parking lot at one forty-five.

"A pelting rain puddled the parking lot as we sat in Mr. Kingford's Mercedes discussing my situation. He advised me to stay as calm as possible and to tell the truth.

"Lieutenant Murphy was seated behind an imposing mahogany desk. I couldn't remember ever having seen anyone so unbelievably huge. He pointed at two chairs in front of the desk and introduced himself in a voice that belied his immense stature. I repressed a smile and began to relax.

"There were no pleasantries.

"The lieutenant asked if Mrs. Beckerley's diamond ring had been on her finger when I found her. I informed him it had not. He said I seemed quite sure, and I assured him I was. He wanted to know why. I told him there was no doubt in my mind because when she had it on I couldn't keep my eyes off it. A smirk slowly crept across his face as his soft, silky voice gloated, 'Oh, you liked the ring?' I tried to stay calm and couldn't wait to tell the truth as I responded that of course I liked it. Then I looked him squarely in the eye and said, 'If any female denied she wouldn't die, at the very least, for that ring, she'd be lying.' Obviously not pleased but satisfied with my answer, he asked when I last remembered seeing the ring. I couldn't give him an exact date. It had been quite awhile—at least two months.

"Next he asked about the missing money. I was no help there either. I could only repeat what I had told the two officers the night Mrs. Beckerley died.

"Mr. Kingford and I were dismissed.

"I thought more and more about the two thousand dollars. I knew it had to be somewhere in Mrs. Beckerley's desk and couldn't understand why the police hadn't been able to find it.

"I decided to ask Mr. Kingford if it would be possible to have an antique dealer go through the desk. I telephoned and told him of my interest in antiques and that, while my knowledge was limited, I felt Mrs. Beckerley's desk could very possibly have a secret compartment. He thanked me and said it was worth a try.

"Not long afterward, Mr. Kingford called to say our antique dealer had found the two thousand dollars.

"Relief consumed me.

"He went on to say we were not out of the woods yet though. The ring had not been found and one more search of the house was planned for the following morning. He asked if I'd like to join him, Lieutenant Murphy and three of his offices for that one last look. I asked where I could meet him. I didn't want to go alone.

"We all arrived at ten the next morning.

"Accompanied by one of the officers, I began my search in Mrs. Beckerley's bedroom. As I started toward the dresser, the officer let out a long, low whistle. I turned. Lying on the spring under the corner of the mattress he held in his hand was a gun—a toy gun. Mrs. Beckerley must have put it there in fear of an intruder. I had had no idea she'd been so frightened.

"I thought about her affectionately as my eyes wandered around the room.

"I returned to the dresser and looked down at the jewelry box; it seemed so alone and abandoned. Nostalgia filled my heart as I picked it up. I turned to put it on the bed when another officer barreled through the door bumping into me. Earrings, bracelets, rings, pins went flying, and the jewelry box crashed to the floor. Like a quick spurt of heat lightening something flashed. We all looked up. Then I saw it—sparkling, innocent, unassuming—happy to have landed on the soft Oriental rug by Mrs. Beckerley's bed.

"I bent down and picked it up. As I held the lovely diamond reverently in the palm of my hand, I was filled with the quiet peace of a rippling, mountain stream. I smiled through tears glistening in the sunlight for I knew Mrs. Beckerley had shared my peace and was gone.

"We never would have found the ring if she hadn't pushed that officer into me. The false bottom in her jewelry box would have remained a secret forever.

"Downstairs in the foyer, Mr. Kingford took both my hands and asked if there was anything in the house Mrs. Beckerley had said I could have. I told him she hadn't but, if possible, I would like to buy the antique chair she had put up in my room. He told me he knew Mrs. Beckerley would want me to have it, considering all I had been through. But it would have to be appraised and go through probate with the rest of her estate. He did say he would do all he could to get the chair for me at a price he hoped I could afford.

"We said goodbye. I never expected to hear from him again.

"But, to my surprise, I did. In the meantime, my pen and I explored the world of words trying to leave the past behind and move on to what was waiting."

Emma removes a piece of paper from her pocket.

"It's so rewarding when words come together in just the right way.

Footprints linger in sandy earth,
Abandoned to solitude
By a lonesome figure
Disappearing 'round the bend
In a quiet country road,
Where calm and stillness
Make the grass seem greener,
Though veiled with settled dust,
The sky seem brighter though
Clothed in its old blue dress.

Quietly waits the crumbling wall
Whose stones were huddled
By ancient hands.
A special spot to sit awhile
And visit with feelings
So long awry, to ponder
The question why all must die,
Then marvel at the maple's ken,
'When winter's o'er,
I'll bloom again.'

"Many months later, Mr. Kingford called to say he had the chair for me at the incredible price of ten dollars. It would have been a bargain at three hundred.

"The chair sits in front of one of my bedroom windows. As I walk by it, I often wonder if Mrs. Beckerley comes to visit me now and then.

"Think she does, Luke?"

Emma returns the poem to her pocket, folds her hands in her lap and rocks, soothed by the songs of the floor and the little purple finch.

She's sure he's been listening and hopes he'll respond soon. Her time is running out.

That's one cool lady. I knew she'd handle it.

It rains throughout the night and continues to pour this morning, obliterating the view beyond Emma's window.

She snuggles deeper under her quilt.

We'll have to stay inside today. Wouldn't it be nice to spend the entire day right here in my cozy hideaway?

She finally opens her eyes, but makes no effort to move. She sighs, knowing she must.

Every day each move becomes more of an effort.

Emma makes the effort.

While going through her morning routine, she decides she'll put on her bright yellow sweater as a substitute for the sunshine. Before going downstairs, she sits in her cheery yellow chair for awhile watching images of Edgewood amble through the rain coming down outside her window.

It rained like this that Labor Day weekend Lois and I went back to Edgewood. Everyone seemed so happy to see us. I looked for you Sim, but you weren't around. Later that evening when you walked into the bar, I felt my neck heat up. Lois said, "You've seen him." Oh yes, I'd seen you. And everyone else saw the blotchy red spots that always blossomed on my neck whenever you appeared on the scene. It was kind of a joke up there, wasn't it?

I even remember the song coming from the jukebox—*Chances Are* by Johnny Mathis. You asked me to dance, and we spent the entire evening together. You didn't bring up July and neither did I.

The next night the moon came out, and we took a ride in the speedboat over to our special island where the old deserted castle stood waiting. I was frightened, like I'd always been when we climbed up onto the parapets to sit high above the ambling St. Lawrence River. You reached for my hand and told me I was special, that you'd never met anyone quite like me. Somehow I knew you were leading up to something I wouldn't like. And I didn't. San Francisco General had accepted your application for an internship. You were leaving for California in two weeks.

How sweet you were, dear Sim, promising to write. You continued to hold my hand as we watched the river float by, silence egging on my tears glistening in the moonlight. My hand had felt so warm and safe inside of yours, but suddenly I wanted it back.

It was then I admitted watching you and your mother in the gazebo that evening back in July as you both gazed out over the water waiting for the sun to disappear behind the horizon. I suspected you'd written and told her about me—that I was catholic. I'm sure you felt she ought to know since she'd lived her entire life hating what she referred to as papists. You joked about it but knew deep in your heart the word papist was never uttered in jest.

My poor Sim, you had to deal with her tears and mine too.

Well, I guess I could have prevented those tears if I'd only known the difference between love and romance. But how could I? Back then, unfortunately, I was filled with youthful, naïve dreams of amoré and idealism. But, was it so unfortunate? If I hadn't dreamed those dreams, would I have ventured beyond the safety of home and friends? Probably not, and what a shame that would have been.

Would I have discovered that love's portrait depicts more than dancing in the moonlight, love songs, kisses and flattering words of love? Maybe. Or would I have found out too late that sacrifice is the canvas upon which the portrait is painted?

Emma sighs, summons the strength to get out of her chair and goes down the hall to the elevator.

After enjoying a special treat of pancakes, Emma goes in search of Catherine. She finds her in the sitting room making her people there more comfortable, wrapping sweaters across bony shoulders, placing woolen shawls over arthritic knees. Emma beckons from the doorway, and Catherine joins her in the foyer.

"Catherine, this rain is not going to stop today or even tomorrow. My bones have reassured me of that. Do you think you can find a spot somewhere in this capacious mansion where Luke and I can enjoy a little privacy? I mustn't lose time or continuity."

Catherine considers the possibilities. "Sure and if no one is using the little sewing room on the second floor, it would be just the thing. And if I lit a fire in the fireplace, you two could be quite cozy up there. Get yourself another cup of coffee and I'll be right back." She starts to leave, then turns, "By the way, Emma, I wish I had the words to tell you how much I admire what you're doin'. Sure and don't ever hesitate to ask if you need my help."

In the dining room Emma pours herself a fresh cup of coffee and saunters over to a table by the window from which, on most days, one can see for miles. Gazing out at the descending deluge, her mind becomes preoccupied with thoughts of where to begin if the little sewing room and a comfy fire turn out to be a reality.

Catherine hurries into the dining room, obviously in search of Emma. A smile as wide as the Grand Canyon lights up her face as she takes Emma's arm.

"Let's go. Luke is upstairs, hopefully enjoyin the heat of a roarin fire."

Emma smiles and says, "Bend down here young lady so I can kiss that soft, pink cheek of yours."

"Aw, gawan, Emma Duprey, sure and it was the least I could do."

But she complies, then escorts Emma up in the elevator but leaves her at the door of the small sewing room.

Emma enters and sits down in the rocker Catherine has placed directly in front of the fire. Luke sits silent and still. He seems to be waiting. Emma leans toward the fire and floats her hands in front of its warmth. What a shame Luke cannot see their rhythm.

She smiles for she knows exactly where she will begin on this cold, damp, rainy day.

"Good morning Luke. It's a terrible day—raining and windy. We're very fortunate Catherine was able to arrange this nice, warm room for us."

Silence prevails as usual, but Emma pushes on.

"Well, Luke, I had another big decision to make. A rather quick one this time. Not as crucial as deciding to leave home. But important nevertheless.

"It was 6:00 PM in the Windsor Café on a hot, steamy evening in August. A soft red hue emanating from exit signs and florescent Budweiser, Miller and Old Milwaukee bar advertisements pervaded its cool, dry atmosphere.

"'Whirr. Whirr. Whirr.'

"An air-conditioner competed with Dean Martin crooning *That's Amoré.* Both competed with the warbling whistle of a burly bartender wiping glasses behind an old mahogany bar.

"The café was empty, with the exception of Maggie, Peg and me. We were sitting in our regular booth by the large bay window that overlooked Windsor's bucolic town common. The beer in front of us was ice cold—hardly visible in the frosty mugs—the pizza so hot it burned our tongues. We unconsciously devoured both as we became ardently enrapt in the gossip of Maynard Aircraft. When the pizza had disappeared and the mugs were empty, we ordered more cold beer. The heat and humidity could wait…we'd tackle the world outside a little later.

"While Maggie and Peg tried to decide what movie we could keep cool in, I tried to decide whether to share with them my renewed interest in Neal. You remember him, Luke, the engineer who pulled imaginary straws out of my hair.

"Both deliberations came to an abrupt end when Neal and Peter, one of the test pilots, sluggishly pushed open the heavy paneled door of the café and flopped into a booth behind us. Maggie and I waved. Peg turned around to delight them with her famous, infectious smile. They wanted to know how come we looked so calm, cool and comfortable. Peg chirped we'd been there awhile. We all expounded on the weather. When there was no more to be said about the steamy hot, sultry humidity that makes Connecticut tobacco grow, the conversation turned to *The Tender Trap*, a play Maynard's theater group had been rehearsing for the past few weeks.

Without warning, Neal got up and pushed in next to Peg. He asked if one of us would like to take part in the play. I asked if he meant to act? To play a role? To portray a character? He replied, 'Why not?' The three of us roared with laughter and assured him emoting upon the boards was not a talent any one of us listed in our repertoires of versatile accomplishments.

"He got down on his knees at the end of the table and begged one of us to *please* rescue the production. We listened as he told his sad tale. The group had been rehearsing since the beginning of May in preparation for performances during the middle two weeks of September. Annabelle, who was to play Sylvia, had informed the director earlier that week she would be leaving in two weeks for Scottsdale, Arizona. She had accepted a position she could not refuse. The group was desperate. At this late date, no one wanted to take on the task of learning so many lines…in addition to all the stage directions.

"Neal expounded on how important it was for him to play Charlie, the leading man. I sympathized as I'd seen him perform lesser roles in a number of productions staged by the Windsor Jesters—a popular theater group in the Hartford area. He was a good actor, and I knew he was trying to build a reputation. Desperately, I wanted to help him. A little voice kept saying, 'Do it, do it.' But I didn't dare. What did I know about acting? I looked at him as he pleaded with sorrowful, doe-like, gray eyes staring directly into mine. Like ice cream sitting in the sun, I melted into an idiot and told him I'd be willing to give it a try. You'd think I had condemned them all to death. When the shock wore off, everyone started talking at once. Neal got off his knees and gave me a little-more-than-friendly kiss. The ice cream continued to melt. Whatever I had to do for the next few weeks was going to be worth every minute.

"The following evening, I took my first step on a road that would extend for miles and miles.

"Mark, the director, greeted me with open arms and thanked me profusely for being there. I assured him I didn't think I'd be much help. He handed me a script and said my first task was to read the play and let him know why I thought Messrs. Shulman and Smith had written it. He hoped I could do that by the following evening. I went home and read the play. I thought about it and decided Shulman and Smith wanted to make people laugh. They understood human beings are seldom touched by anything that is not personally relevant. So they created characters who were every-day people, doing commonplace things, in a very funny way. Mark agreed and assured me I would have no trouble creating a believable Sylvia.

"Rehearsals were held four evenings a week. My mind soon became inundated with Sylvia's lines and stage directions. But something was missing; she was like a little girl's paper doll—dressed, placed where wanted and given words. I began to probe into the mystique of Sylvia's character. Messrs. Shulman and Smith had put words in her mouth, and those I knew. I had to give her a soul; bring her to life. A very difficult task...I kept interjecting myself.

"All aspects of the theater turned out to be much harder than I had anticipated, but I loved the challenge and the involvement. How fortunate for me that fate had sent Neal into the Windsor Café on a hot and steamy evening.

"September arrived, and suddenly it was opening night; rehearsals were over. I shall never ever forget it. I was seated in a chair, shrouded in a deep purple cape. Ken had finished spraying my hair a light brown and was busy applying makeup. He nonchalantly asked, 'So how's Sylvia?' A moment went by. Somewhere, a muscled arm struck the thousand-pound gong of reality.

"In a few hours, I would have to walk onto that stage and convince hundreds of people I was Sylvia. Could I make them understand her, love her, enjoy her? Could I make them laugh? I closed my eyes and silently wailed, '*Oh my god, what have I done?'* If I happened to be lucky enough to put one foot in front of the other and reach the stage, I'd never be able to utter a word. I'd stand there, staring into oblivion.

"I raised my hands and told Ken to stop; I wasn't going on. I remember he said, 'Of course you are. You're only suffering from first-night jitters.' But when I stood up and started to take off the cape he realized I was serious and called Mark, who came running and put his arm around my shoulders. I blurted out that I just couldn't do it. Very softly and in a kind, fatherly manner he told me I had no choice. I stood shaking my head back and forth. Someone went for Neal. He, along with the rest of the cast, came running and tried to convince me the show must go on. Through all the babble I continued to shake my head. Neal took my hand and led me into a small room used for storing scenery. He assured me he knew exactly what I was going through. It had happened to him many times. It happened to everyone in the theater.

"I was numb. I heard his words, and from the depth of my soul I tried desperately to find the courage I needed. But I had forgotten Sylvia's every word. My mind was blank. I knew my name, and I knew I was in the Windsor Theatre...but that was all. Neal continued his logic and his pleas. I covered my face with pale, trembling fingers. Tears, like a cascade of tiny crystal beads, escaped down the backs of my hands. I sobbed and sobbed for I didn't want to let all those wonderful people down, but I had no choice. Sylvia wasn't a deaf mute.

"Neal caressed my cheek and left, saying he'd be back in a minute. Before closing the door he turned and looked at me, then came back and raised my chin with the bent knuckle of his forefinger. 'Now don't panic, okay.'

"When he returned, he asked if I would be willing to let Ken repair and finish my makeup then get into the suit I was to wear in my opening scene. I nodded again. He led me out of the small sanctuary as if I was a frightened little girl. Actually, I was a frightened *big* girl.

"Ken repaired the damage to my makeup; Sue coiffed my hair, and Molly helped me into a sparkling white organdy blouse, placed the skirt of a lovely pink suit over my hips and draped the short, belted jacket across my sagging shoulders. I stood in the wings of the Windsor Theater.

"A lilting, harmonious melody traveled up from the orchestra pit and a hush of anticipation settled over the audience. Two heavy, maroon velvet curtains, edged with gold braid and black fringe, gracefully swished to opposite ends of the stage. Slowly, mysteriously light peeked out from behind a wing chair, glided along the back of a tufted sofa and over the green leaves of a potted plant before illuminating a large tree outside the living room's picture window. As the light continued to miraculously float over tables and across Oriental rugs, those watching slipped from reality into the enchanted, make-believe world of the theater.

"The play began. My friends became...*were* Charlie, Poppy, Joe and Jessica. I stood there mesmerized, watching and listening, unaware I was waiting for Charlie's cue. When it came, I instinctively moved toward the stage. Someone whispered, 'Break a leg,' and I took my first step into the world of live theatre. With open arms, Charlie said, 'Sylvia, Baby!'

"How am I going to describe what happened next? Sylvia stood in the middle of Charlie's living room. All her words were there; she moved where she was supposed to move; her soul shone through.

"As I heard the words that cued Charlie's and my exit, I felt a disappointment I'd often experienced when the music stopped and a dance was through. Backstage, Neal gave me a comforting, warm hug. I received a thumbs-up from everyone else. Dumbfounded by what I had just experienced, I could only smile. No words could have expressed what I was feeling.

"When the first scene ended, the two velvet curtains swished together again. The audience clapped and clapped, then chatted noisily while waiting for the play to continue.

"No one said anything to me. We were all too busy changing outfits for the second scene. I couldn't wait; I had the first line.

"Charlie, Joe and Sylvia sat down at the table in Charlie's living room and waited. Again, with a sweeping swish, the heavy, velvet curtains journeyed toward their separate destinations. Sylvia smiled and said, 'More coffee, anyone?' The scene unfolded, and the play proceeded.

"Sylvia's final appearance came toward the end of the last scene in the third act. She was dressed in a stunning black wool suit with a black mink stole flung over one shoulder. As she was about to deliver her exit line, Sylvia dropped the beautiful mink stole and dragged it across the stage behind her. Charlie rose from the bench he was sitting on. At the door, she turned toward the audience and said, 'Say good luck—because there'll be no more second best for me. I'm going to find me an honest-to-god guy who's looking for an honest-to-god girl. Somewhere in this great city, there must be one!' Head held high, she opened the door and disappeared, continuing to drag the expensive black mink stole across the floor. Sylvia received a standing ovation. When silence prevailed once more, the play continued to its conclusion.

"I wonder, Luke, why I remember those lines. Perhaps I kind of like that '… no more second best for me.'

"Back stage, I was hugged, kissed and hugged again. Speechless, I tried to fathom the reality that I actually had performed on a stage and received deafening applause—applause just for me.

"When the heavy, velvet curtains made their final journey, another standing ovation exploded for the entire cast. It was the thrill of a lifetime and will always stand alone, though labeled many things: fulfilling a commitment, effecting that considered impossible, blossoming talent perhaps, a wisely made decision.

"Don't bother to wonder how the owner of the black mink stole felt when it was being dragged across the floor; she never saw it. The audience enjoyed this particular piece of stage business during every performance but one. The owner of the stole always attended the third night of any performance...she knew the bugs would have been worked out by then.

"As a member of Maynard's theatre group and the Windsor Jesters, I performed in many plays and worked behind the scenes for many more; I loved it all.

"But, my wanderlust wouldn't allow me to remain in one place too long, and I left Hartford to try my luck on the boards of another of life's stages.

"Once in awhile, with words, I visit that unique moment when deafening applause turned me into a sparkling brilliance because it thundered just for me."

Sitting there quietly, it all comes back—the costumes, the makeup, the sets, the music, the play, the wonderful make-believe…the *applause*. Almost reverently Emma unfolds the paper she has taken from the pocket of her sweater and begins to read:

"How still the darkness
And quiet the daisies
Asleep by an old, weathered fence,
Dreaming their dreams
As time journeys on
Toward the waiting dawn,
When they wake
To an ordinary life,
Coaxing smiles
From each saddened face,
Bringing color to ivy
So alone in its vase.

Their petals swallow
The morning dew,
As Sol climbs high
To a cloudless sky,
From whence
Sunbeams chance
Upon a windowpane,
To tarry then dance
Down the old, weathered fence
To rest just a moment
On sweet innocence.

Which sparkles, then glows
In the radiant rays.
All else in the garden
Simply fades, fades away.
Glory reigns for that instant,
'Fore Sol wanders on,
Then lingers for always
In memory,
To be oft recaptured
By blooms plain of mien,
Left behind in their garden
To grow and to dream.

A warm, extraordinary moment
In a simple ordinary life
Lives on, lives on forever,
To remind the sun will shine.
A stirring, memorable moment,
So few, so few
In a lifetime."

Emma rocks and soaks up the warmth of the fire and the nearness of youth. Periodically, Catherine tiptoes in to put fresh logs on the fire, then quietly tiptoes out again. To all outward appearances, Luke seems as far away as ever. Only Emma knows there's a difference—the wind hasn't carried her carefully chosen words over and beyond the top of her mighty mountain.

She smiles; they never reached the wind.

Theater, poetry—yeah, I dig the poetry.

But the rain has stopped. Emma's old bones had been mistaken. In the bright autumn sunshine, leaves of red and gold gracefully sway from limbs of trees standing tall along hidden trails and dirt-paved roads.

Bundled in her heavy Irish-knit sweater and wrapped in an afghan, Emma savors her best-loved season—that time of year when depleted energy returns, snowflakes gather not far off, firewood inches higher and higher up the side of the old red barn, and tourists, some from as far away as California, come to experience the brilliance of autumn in New England. She smiles thinking how lucky she is to have a front-row seat.

Emma detects a different sound and turns to see Catherine walking toward her escorted by a gentleman in a handsome tweed jacket. It's the tap, tap of his cane she's heard. Emma wonders who he is and feels a twinge of uneasiness. If he's come because of Luke, she wants no interference. As they approach, Emma stiffens. Catherine introduces her to Dr. Billings, Luke's psychiatrist.

"Good morning Mrs. Duprey."

Emma nods but says nothing. The doctor continues, "Luke's mother is quite enthusiastic about what you are trying to do for her son. She asked me to pay you a visit. So here I am. Would it be too much of an imposition to ask that you share your theory with me?"

Emma stops rocking and sits up straight. She looks directly at Dr. Billings. "I've only a hope with a prayer behind it, Doctor." she says before confidently describing the tack she is taking. The doctor allows she certainly isn't doing Luke any harm. He pauses, then asks, "Would you mind if I joined you?"

"Not at all, but I do feel Luke should be aware of your presence."

"I wholeheartedly agree."

Catherine has been observing from a distance. She notices Emma beckon and comes running.

"Catherine would you please find Dr. Billings a chair and then go up and get Luke."

"Certainly, I'll be right back."

A heavy silence prevails until Catherine brings Dr. Billings a chair. It continues when she leaves for Luke.

"Well, here we are, Emma. Sure and would anyone be carin' for a cup of coffee before I'm on my way?"

"Not for me thank you. Dr. Billings?"

"Oh no, I'm fine, thank you."

"Luke, Dr. Billings is visiting today. He's going to stay for my story."

Emma senses Luke is not as relaxed as usual. She begins to rock. Staring out at her mighty mountain, she silently prays it will share its strength. When fifteen minutes go by in silence, Dr. Billings rises, smiles at Emma and suggests he come back another time.

Emma bows her head but makes no other reply.

The gravel on the driveway growls as the doctor drives away.

"You didn't seem comfortable, Luke, so I thought I'd wait on the story."

But she waits no longer.

"Motivation is our subject today, Luke."

She hesitates for just a second or two.

"Every spring it happened—the aroma of lilacs, the golden hue of jonquils, a tiny striped chipmunk chirping high upon a fence post. How I loved that time of year. Still do. But in my younger years I couldn't wait to jump into a boat and motor across a deep blue lake bored by winter's stillness or dive into a cold, salty surf. And I longed to answer the call of strange, enchanting cities beckoning from far, far away. Oh yes, I yearned to answer all those harbingers that interrupted my winter lethargy, that hinted the cold north wind had gone where cold north winds go and suggested the warmth of summer waited just around the corner. They amplified whispers of 'Come. Come.'

"Well, Luke, in the spring of 1956 my friend Maggie was going. Her plans had been made for some time. In just a few days her dream would tumble into reality—two weeks in San Francisco.

"Maggie's mother, Peg and I never moved until her plane was a tiny dot on the horizon. We each silently wondered if we'd ever see her again. San Francisco was, after all, on the other side of the world. At least that's how it seemed to us as we stood there on Bradley Field's observation roof watching the wide-winged eagle carry off our excited, curious, little bluebird.

"The weekend we expected Maggie home, I received a letter from her. When I picked it out of the mailbox a tingle of excitement flew into my fingertips. I tore open the envelope. It fell to the floor as I began to read the familiar writing. I stood there in the foyer stunned; Maggie wasn't coming home.

"She wrote that her letter of resignation to Dr. Bagnall would be waiting for him on Monday morning. It had been a traveling companion to the letter I squeezed in my hand. I continued to read. She was working in the ER at San Francisco General and was sharing an apartment with two roommates. I asked myself how all this could have happened in two weeks. The last line read, 'Resign. I'll call.' I thought, just like that. Resign?

"Retrieving the envelope, I ran up the stairs to the third floor. My thoughts raced and bumped into each other like dodgems at an amusement park. This I hadn't expected. I called Peg and asked if she had received a letter from Maggie. I can hear her as if it were yesterday. 'Yeah, I sure did. Is she nuts? I'm not going to resign. And I'm certainly not going out to California.'

"We talked for about an hour and a half. Poor Peg, she simply couldn't believe I'd pack up and move on to another of life's stages, just like that... particularly one so far away. She made it plain her life would continue to play in Bloomfield.

"Maggie called as she promised she would, and we made plans—exciting plans.

"A few weeks later Mama and Daddy stood on the observation roof of Boston's Logan Airport and watched a tiny dot disappear into the distant horizon. Everyone else hurried off to meet the challenges of a new day while they remained to stare at the empty blue expanse high above their heads. They told me they'd stayed for a long time silently wondering if they'd ever see me again.

"While they watched, I sat next to a window thousands and thousands of feet above them, not exactly frightened, more uneasy. I thought about looking down but knew I wasn't anywhere near ready for that. So I just stared at the seat in front of me asking if maybe I'd been too hasty.

"I realized how lucky I was to have a place to live but couldn't help wondering what my prospects were for finding a good job. San Francisco sounded pretty expensive to me.

"Mama popped into my mind, and I hoped she wasn't too unhappy. I knew Chocolate was secretly thrilled and wished he was the one starting out on this adventure.

"Bumpity bump, the dodgems were at it again. I was grateful no one was sitting beside me; I could never have carried on a coherent conversation.

"Without warning my stomach landed on my instep, and I screamed. No one else did. A very pretty and perky stewardess sat down next to me. She explained we had hit an air pocket, and I shouldn't worry, it happened now and then. Her smile and offer of a cup of coffee soothed my apprehension and helped bring back my color. She asked if I'd been enjoying the view. I hoped my smile didn't appear as false as it felt. When she returned with the coffee, I thanked her and began to stare into the still, black liquid. I saw the plane land and me step down onto solid ground. Out of habit, I added sugar, and the comforting images rippled away.

"Hours and miles went by as I tried to read or take a nap, but my eyes kept wandering toward the window. I watched the clouds roll by. Sometimes they made me think of smoke billowing from a burning building. Other times they seemed like fog hovering over a calm sea. I thought of Mrs. Beckerley. Perhaps they weren't clouds at all but floating, graceful spirits happy to be on their way home. As I daydreamed, three roaring propellers on the upper edge of a sparkling silver wing cut through the smoke, the fog, the spirits. An annoying little voice, droning along with the steady roar, kept insisting, 'We're flying non-stop. These roaring, spinning blades are only man-made; they're going to give out sooner or later.' I imagined the plane descending in flames, and fear gripped my soul. I forced myself to fantasize what it would be like to walk across the Golden Gate Bridge toward a mysterious Shangri-la—the bridge its magnificent foyer. My imagination being what it is, the annoying little voice faded away.

"The perky stewardess tapped me on the shoulder, dissipating my Shangri-la. She pointed out we were flying over Yosemite and I really should look down at the view. I took her advice and peaked behind the gleaming, silver wing. Shadows that looked like patchwork quilts sewn with multiple pieces of pine-green material waltzed gracefully up and down the mountains. As they dipped and twirled, a bright, blinding light abruptly burst forth as if someone had lit two dozen gigantic fourth-of-July sparklers. I gasped, then smiled. The sun had decided to sit a moment on the top of Yosemite Falls.

"A kind of calm spread through me as I continued to gaze at the miniature trees, puddles of water and waltzing shadows. I felt sorry I hadn't looked down before. The smoke, the fog, the spirits hadn't been there all the while. I couldn't help but think how cruel fear is for depriving us of the beauty and wonders of a world forever waiting.

"In spite of this newly found state of relaxation, I breathed a sigh of relief when the Captain's voice announced we were approaching San Francisco Airport and 'Fasten Your Seatbelt' flashed above my head. The plane finally bumped and skidded along the runway. I remember sitting as stiff as a board, my arms and hands rigid as they pressed against the arms of my seat. When the plane thankfully came to a halt, I relaxed and happily followed my fellow passengers out the door and down a portable staircase. The Captain stood at the bottom waiting to bid us all adieu. As my foot touched solid ground, he smiled and said, 'You certainly look relieved.' I replied, 'Oh, I am. I've been watching those propellers for eight hours. They're only man-made and are bound to call it quits sooner or later.' He laughed, 'We're going to gas up and start right back.' I grinned, 'Better you than me.'

"Maggie was standing on the apron, her blue eyes twinkling, her arms frantically waving as I ran toward her."

What's she looking for? What I'm listening for?

Emma pauses and wraps the afghan tighter around her knees. She feels a little tired and lapses into her own private thoughts.

Dear, dear Maggie, you never knew you weren't the only one to help make up my mind to come to San Francisco. Sim, too, had a hand in that decision. He called the week before he left for California and invited me to join him for the weekend at his sister Janet's in Springfield. That call made your suggestion to resign much more plausible than it otherwise might have been.

I often think how welcoming Janet's freshly cut daisies were when I found them on my bedside table.

It was a wonderful weekend, even though Sim and I didn't have a lot of time together. It turned out to be a whirlwind of dining, dancing and taking Janet's little boy David to the circus.

Little David, little David, you must be an old man by now. I will never forget that Sunday morning as I hurried to change the sheets. You suddenly appeared in the doorway, and I asked if you'd like to help. You looked at me so innocently and wanted to know if I was going to marry your Uncle Sim. What was it I said? Something like your Uncle Sim hadn't asked me. With such naïve candor you replied, "Maybe he won't 'cause you're not pretty enough." My poor heart—it leaped and, I think, stopped for an instant. I know it did.

But, dear Maggie, as you know, I came anyway, in spite of my lack of good looks.

I wonder if I should tell Luke about Sim—probably not. Romantic aspirations had bowed to realism long before Luke's generation. No, Sim will remain my secret.

Her reverie has almost put Emma to sleep. But she straightens up.

Did one of her ethereal friends give her a nudge?

Where am I?

She smiles and looks over at Luke.

"Oh! Let me see now. Where was I? Oh yes.

"A borrowed, sand-colored Volkswagen convertible—top down of course—waited patiently in the crowded parking lot while Maggie and I, arms wrapped around each other, silently hurried toward it. The chatter began as soon as we hopped in. I'm sure we sounded like a whirlwind day on Wall Street; we couldn't talk fast enough or loud enough. Neither of us could hear what the other was saying. Laughter exploded into the air, the excitement electric as Maggie sped off. I wonder to this day how my friend ever managed to drive.

"We raced up the highway in the little sand convertible, our hair blowing in the wind, our eyes squinting in the bright sunlight. The air had a sparkling, fresh scent of sheets plucked from a clothesline after hours spent blowing in the wind. Where were the pines, the maples, the oaks standing guard by the side of the road? The sky seemed an unending expanse of blue. I wondered why I didn't just float right up onto a wispy, white cloud. I could see for miles and miles and miles. Had my head been attached to ball bearings, I couldn't have seen everything there was to see.

"Maggie's eyes paralleled the color of the sky and sparkled with laughter as she tried to watch me as well as the road. Houses, huddled together closer than fans at a football game, came into view, and I sensed we were nearing the city. Maggie pointed out Candlestick Park to my right, and I just couldn't believe it all.

"We took a quick tour around the city before Maggie headed for the crookedest street in the world—Lombard Street; I was going to live on Lombard Street.

"The little sand Volkswagon sidled up to a curbstone. Maggie looked at me and chirped, 'We're here.' We got out and walked toward an arch in the opening of a white stucco wall. Maggie waved me through, and I walked into a courtyard where water cascaded up and down in the center of a fountain singing its melody to colorful asters, geraniums and daisies playfully dancing beneath it. Waltzing around the courtyard's outer edges, more white, yellow and green blossoms blew scents of jasmine, lily and mint off their petals in welcome.

"Eight white stucco apartments—two up and two down on each side—surrounded the courtyard. We climbed the stairs to the first floor apartment on the right...Apartment B. Maggie's two roommates, Evie and Laura greeted us with open arms. Their smiles were as broad and bright as the gleaming silver wings that brought me to this enchanting spot—the City by the Bay. I stepped into their living room and knew I was entering a brand new world. I wondered what it held for me.

"Outside and beyond the stucco walls, San Francisco's steep hills were peppered with cable cars traveling up and down, up and down like colorful, busy ladybugs—each cable car a story in itself. One muscular operator entertained his passengers with a rhyme as they went down each hill. His deep baritone voice would ring out, 'No sparkin on Larkin,' as he pulled the heavy, metal lever that controlled his speed and direction.

"From almost every section of the City, part or all of the red-orange Golden Gate Bridge sparked an excited effervescence deep within each captivated viewer.

"San Francisco was a city of impeccable charm and grace. A perfect hostess, she offered shopping, restaurants, fabulous hotels and unbelievable views. Her sparkling lights enhanced the enchantment. And her loud, melodious sounds added stimulation to the atmosphere—all the while tantalizing the prisoners watching and listening from their cells on Alcatraz Island.

"Of course, I didn't know about any of this that first day as I sat on the soft leather sofa. I sensed, though, from the attire, speech and frank, open faces looking into mine that I was about to embark on a far more sophisticated stage than I had ever played upon before. My feelings of apprehension began to fade. My life was about to change. I would no longer be protected, nor restricted, by maples, oaks and pines. They were in another world where New England huddled with years-old tradition. Here life was going to be audacious, free, expansive, inviting and enticing. I couldn't wait to begin.

"My first step was to unpack.

"Maggie had always shared a room with Evie who had come to the city from the Virgin Islands. So, I moved in with Laura who hailed from Wethersfield, Connecticut. She and I hit it off from the very beginning.

"The apartment had two bedrooms, a large living room, a satisfactory kitchen and one bathroom. It suited us all to a tee. Upstairs three budding IBM executives lived in Apartment F, and we all joyfully shared our lives and resources. It would be difficult to find a more unique and convivial arrangement.

"I'll never forget Billy's first dinner party.

"He and I rode the same bus to work every morning as we both had jobs in the same building on California. He'd pick me up on his way down the back staircase. One particular Friday morning he knocked on the kitchen door and informed me that he wasn't going to work. He needed the entire day to prepare for a dinner party he was giving that evening.

"When I returned home late in the afternoon, I went directly upstairs to see how Billy was progressing with his dinner. He was totally frazzled—practically in tears when he blurted out that his spaghetti was an utter disaster.

"Unfortunately, he had misinterpreted his cookbook and tried to simmer the spaghetti all day. Poor guy he'd spent his entire time adding water to keep the sides of the pan free of gooey starch. I removed the lid and immediately replaced it. Never had I seen such a mess. I told him to throw it all out—including the pan. I broke it to him as gently as I could that the sauce is cooked all day—the spaghetti only ten minutes.

"My friend was miserable and wanted to chuck the evening along with the spaghetti. But I told him to carry on, make the salad and garlic bread, then set his table. Les femmes downstairs would take care of the rest. As I turned to leave, I asked if any red-blooded Italians were expected. He shook his head. I sighed with relief and hurried down the back staircase. Laura had a delicious, super quick recipe for spaghetti sauce...but not for Italians.

"Billy's dinner party was a great success thanks to the combined efforts of friends in apartments B and F.

"The following morning, I lay out in the courtyard attempting to darken my tan when the air suddenly filled with the strains of *Yellow Bird*—my favorite song at the time. I looked up and saw Billy smiling through the window. He raised his left thumb in the air, and I returned his smile.

"Our lives around that courtyard will forever make my memory laugh, and our lives beyond it are well worth a smile or two. Maggie took care of patients at San Francisco General, Evie handled the affairs of her insurance company executive, Laura calculated blood counts in the laboratory of a doctor's office. I typed and took shorthand at the Domain Corporation.

"I didn't stay at Domain very long, however. I liked my co-workers and supervisor Mr. Allen, the Project Manager of a pipeline being constructed between the United States and Canada. Unfortunately for me, Mr. Allen spent most of his time in the field. I hated to give up my magnificent view from the tenth floor of the Domain Building, but I couldn't stand the boredom.

"I found another position as secretary to the foreign-investment vice president of a banking institution in the middle of the City's financial district.

"The location turned out to be nothing short of perfection for a young, single, eligible female. Particularly as it was situated around the corner from Apoli's, a cosmopolitan bar patronized by most of the district's young executives. It was a long way from the Windsor Café...in more ways than one.

"I spent many a Friday evening getting acquainted with some of San Francisco's more interesting specimens of the male population. One such charming character turned out to be an aspiring actor. My love of acting had not diminished, and I shared with him my hope of an eventual career in the theatre. He strongly encouraged me, as did Laura and Maggie. I ended up taking drama lessons with Mara Alexander Craig, a well known, highly respected instructor of the performing arts for stage and screen in the San Francisco Bay Area.

"Mara used the improvisational method. She would sit regally in her throne-like chair. In front of her, as if protection from the world, stood a black, square table on which rested a black, silver-headed cane. She would bellow out a name or names, and those students would quickly proceed to the stage. Mara would then unfold her plot.

"I remember one in particular. In her low, frog-like voice, Mara demanded, 'Emma and Frank up—NOW.' We all but flew up onto the stage...then waited like two, immobile soldiers standing guard at Buckingham Palace until *the voice* was heard again, 'Emma, you and your fiance´ are entering the foyer of the Fairmont Hotel. You are dressed in a floor length, heavy satin gown. It's deep rich garnet color accentuates your beautiful white hair freshly coiffed into a magnificent French twist and sprinkled with tiny garnet-colored jewels. A mink stole of cocoa hue graces your shoulders. Your long, delicate neck glows with the pearls of an ancient necklace, which once enhanced the creamy throat of the Duchess of Windsor. The pearls were placed in your beautifully manicured hands as you sipped champagne in the back seat of your fiance's Rolls Royce. You're on your way to the Fairmont Hotel to celebrate your engagement.

"'As you stroll through the elegant lobby, your shoe rolls on what feels like a small pebble, and you fall to the floor. Your pearls are rolling in every direction.'

"'Tap. Tap. Tap.'

"The familiar sound of a black cane on a black table—our cue to begin. As long as we were believable, the cane lay dormant. The instant we were not, it sprang to life and the scene was over. We lasted about ten minutes that day with everyone in stitches.

"Mara had an aversion to my Boston accent and referred me to her speech therapist. I was grateful his endeavors weren't entirely successful. Secretly, I loved all the attention. When I said, 'I parked the car in Harvard yard,' everyone else heard, 'I pahked the cah in Hahvahd Yahd.' I was constantly asked to repeat the phrase. Finally, no requests, just, 'Say it Emma.'

"All my friends assured me if it hadn't been for me, no one would have understood John F. Kennedy when he ran for the presidency in 1960.

"Mara was never satisfied with the therapist's efforts but didn't press it. She was pleased with my work and spent a great deal of time with me. But we did have our differences. I aspired to high drama; she kept steering me toward comedy.

"One very exciting evening in the middle of November, she gave me the opportunity to perform in front of a number of Hollywood directors who often searched out talent among Mara's students. For weeks, Judy, a fellow aspiring actor, and I rehearsed a mother-daughter scene from the play *Dark At The Top of The Stairs*. In context, the scene was high drama—out of context pure comedy. But Mara had kept that fact a deep, dark secret.

"The night of the performance, Judy and I played the scene for its most dramatic effect. Panic seeped into our souls when we heard laughter drifting up from the blackness stretching out before us. We managed to pull ourselves together and finish the scene. *How* will forever be a mystery. You can imagine our surprise when we received a standing ovation.

"Backstage Mara was waiting to explain why she hadn't shared the fact that out of context the scene was high comedy. She said she had wanted to promote my comic talent and knew I would never have agreed to play the mother if I'd known. She was right. Then Mara Craig smiled—a rare occasion—and said that one of the directors had already inquired about me. He thought my timing for comedy was excellent.

"But I did not want to be a comedienne.

"My secret dream was to play Blanche in *A Streetcar Named Desire*. And so it remained…a dream. Mara was right again—talent hovered, but I didn't have the inner freedom necessary to be a good dramatic actress. I had been blessed with a natural timing for comedy.

"I hoped my teacher was wrong, and I continued studying with her. However, that disappointing evening was the closest I ever came to any possibility of having a glamour photo on the cover of *Photoplay* or *Modern Screen*.

"I loved the theatre, and it helped me to expand what little inner freedom I did have. It also reinforced my belief that we become what we choose to absorb from the quantity and quality of the world we allow ourselves to experience."

Emma retrieves the piece of paper in her pocket and reads it to Luke:

"Into a silent,
Ebony void
A stranger speaks.
I listen from what
Seems a long way away.
The voice is familiar.
Is it mine?
It was once.

Why do I hide while
The stranger conveys
Her words of love
That are not mine,
Written for someone
Who is not me
Nor will ever be?

I hear the words I long
To say but never could.
Uttered by a stranger,
In truth myself,
Released from a shared,
Imprisoning cage,
Now free to be
Instead of me.
Oh, the wonder
Of the stage."

Returning the poem to her pocket, Emma experiences a sense of achievement on this bright and glorious afternoon. She feels Luke's faith, his trust. She knows she made the right decision in keeping silent while Dr. Billings was here.

Before Catherine takes him back to his room, she says to Luke, "I'm going to give you something to think about tonight. A long time ago a man named Thomas Lovell Beddoes wrote a poem he called Dream-Pedlary. There is one line in that poem I have never forgotten. It asks a question, which I ask you, "If there were dreams to sell, what would you buy?"

Catherine takes Luke up to his room and settles him comfortably in a chair by the window. She puts a glass of water on the table beside it.

"Sure and I'll be back when its time for dinner, Luke. Ring your bell if you need me fore then. Bye, bye now lad."

I'm glad I let the old lady in.

Luke stares into his dark abyss and reflects on why it doesn't seem as black anymore.

She's brought color—roaring, greenish-gray waves, silver airplanes soaring through clouds (or maybe ghosts), a woman dressed in black dragging mink, red velvet curtains travelling across a stage.

Yet, it's not color stirs the old blood. That warmth flows because of tempo. I can feel her rhythm. But there's more. I know there's more.

She's trying to tell me something. What? And why?

What was it she said a few days ago? Nothing gets done except by someone who has something special inside him that is greater than the situation he's in. Yeah, that's it, that's it.

She's telling me—what? what?

Without warning, a screen saver of motorcycles, musical notes, and pretty faces float in front of him. He watches as they change into the undulating words "…lead us past the roaring waves, hope holding tight our hand."

He sees her hand reach out to him, just her hand.

Who are you anyway?

What was that?

All is still.

There it is again.

Luke leans his ear into the darkness, but hears nothing.

He waits.

Just my imagination I guess.

What was it she asked me? If dreams were for sale, which one would I buy?

I don't know. My brain is like an old piece of rusted machinery.

Yeah, but she's oiled it. Think.

What dream would I buy?

I don't know; I don't know.

Weeell, yeah, maybe I do. Maybe I'd buy that dream of me riding my bike out to a field where I sit on a stone wall and...What? Shit, I can't make it out, but whatever it is, it's important to this dream.

When it's clearer, that's the dream I'll buy.

The colder wind of mid October has coaxed its warmer relative to fly away with the birds and the butterflies. Rocking chairs and wicker tables have been put away for the winter. The porch looks lonely. The colder wind feels cheated, having nothing to tumble about. It envies its warmer cousin the fun of watching Catherine scamper after white wicker tables and pretty linen tea napkins.

Invigorated by the blustery air, Catherine bounces into the dining room and sits down at Emma's table.

"Sure and I hate to be the bearer of bad news Emma, but the porch furniture was sent to the cellar early this mornin'."

Emma sighs, obviously disappointed—but not for long.

"Catherine, do you think perhaps the little sewing room would be available today?"

"I've already checked himself and sure it seems the room is open to anyone on a first-come-first-serve basis. I took the liberty of puttin' your knittin' on one of the rockin' chairs and the lad's red sweater on the other."

"Thank you Catherine. I don't know what I'd do without you."

"Aw gawan, me fine lady."

Emma laughs, "Well, I'm finished here; I really don't feel much like toast this morning. Maybe I'll just saunter up there right now."

Upon stepping out of the elevator, Emma smiles pleased with the aroma of a fire she knows Catherine has lit for Luke and her to enjoy. Her small steps hurry down the hall to the sewing room where she's invited in by the fire and the pale blue yarn waiting on creamy bone needles. She picks up her knitting and stares into the dancing flames. Sim's face stares back at her. It's his sad face that brings her back to San Francisco.

She speaks again to his memory.

"I'll bet I sat on the sofa for over an hour trying to find enough courage to call you at San Francisco General.

"I didn't think anyone was ever going to answer, but finally you said, 'Hello,' and I answered, 'Don't forget the *Salems* for Sim.' You remembered our private joke about the cigarettes. How relieved I was to hear the pleasure in your voice.

"You didn't have a lot of free time. But when you did, we took advantage of every minute, riding cable cars, investigating back alleys in China Town, drinking beer at the Red Garter and strolling leisurely across the Golden Gate Bridge. Didn't we love that bridge?

"Once in awhile you had a whole weekend. Remember? We either climbed Yosemite Falls, snuggled in sleeping bags at Shasta Dam or skied in Donner Pass. I particularly remember the time we drove down through the Big Sur to dine at Nepenthe standing high on a cliff above the beautiful, blue Pacific. Orson Welles had built it for Rita Hayworth. It was so romantic."

Emma's smile disappears when a log breaks. In the furious, hissing flames Sim now sits across from her in the bar at the Top of the Mark.

"Do you remember, Sim, the profound silence that came over the room. Your face told me something extraordinary had happened. I turned and watched Marilyn Monroe drift toward me wrapped in a full length, white fur boa. Never in my life had I ever seen anyone more beautiful. It seems like only yesterday I saw that face, not way back in 1960.

"I think you said something like, 'She's beautiful but I wouldn't want to spend the rest of my life with her.' And what did I say? 'Like visiting New York City but not wanting to live there?'

"Then you reached for my hand and how tenderly you said, 'But I would like to spend the rest of my life with you in this beautiful City by the Bay.'

"I was taken a little off guard, and you asked if I'd heard what you said.

"Oh I'd heard but hadn't anticipated a proposal—not just yet. I loved San Francisco but didn't plan to live there for the rest of my life. It hadn't occurred to me that you would want to stay in California. I didn't expect your answer when I asked if there was any room for negotiation as to where we would live. I remember your exact words, 'Where else? You certainly wouldn't want to go back to New England would you?'

"For months I waged war with you on one side New Hampshire on the other, till I finally realized I couldn't abandon New England any more than I could jump off the Golden Gate Bridge. Nor could you abandon your beloved San Francisco. Sacrifice had never come up before.

"The war ended.

"We said goodbye on a balmy evening in October looking out over the slow, sparkling movement of San Francisco Bay as it flowed impervious beneath our Golden Gate Bridge. I was remembering another moonlit night when I watched the rhythmic movement of the St. Lawrence River flowing slowly below our perch high on the parapet. On both occasions, I'm sure you were watching the slow movement of tears flowing sadly down my cheeks".

Catherine comes into the room with Luke. Then silently goes on her way.

Emma continues to knit a few rows on her sweater before casually asking, "Well, Luke, have you thought of a dream you'd like to buy?" As usual, she doesn't expect an answer. She just hopes he has, for her time is running out.

With a hint of nostalgia in her voice, she just starts talking, almost as if she were talking to herself.

"Life buzzed along, busy as an industrious honey bee. I traveled up and down the hills and dales of San Francisco and along California's glorious countryside. I can only describe those days as joyous, romantic, frightening and frivolous.

"But there's no adjective to describe how I felt the day Maggie packed her car and drove off to the open plains of Montana—such a restless soul had my friend. I hated to see her leave but had no desire to follow.

"Evie's mother arrived from the Virgin Islands for a six-month visit, and she and Evie moved across the bay to Berkeley. Laura and I found a smaller apartment on Twin Peaks with a spectacular view of the city. We were happy there but missed our pals in Apartment F.

"Another Maggie lived in the apartment next door. We became great friends and shared food, stories, trips, secrets, clothes, as all friends will. That friendship lasted all our lives.

"Sharing—what a comforting word. It brings to mind one particular, very special Friday evening. Maggie, Laura and I were all running hither and yon in an effort to make me look my ultimate best for the upcoming evening. I had a mysterious date.

"We finally were all satisfied that I looked perfect in my own black dress, Maggie's brand new black peau-de-soir shoes and Laura's cultured-pearl necklace aglow around my neck. Gracefully falling from my ears were the matching pearl earrings.

"The three of us nervously paced back and forth, back and forth, a scent of Chanel No. 5—Laura's on me—drifting through the air. It's a good thing the tall, handsome chauffeur showed up when he did or my hairdo would have been ruined with all the poking in and pulling out.

"I gasped when the doorbell shrieked. Maggie looked at Laura, Laura looked at Maggie, and they both stared at me. It shrieked again. I breathed in deeply, opened the door and, after one last, comforting look at my friends, followed the stiff-shouldered, liveried young man down the stairs out to a sleek, black, intimidating limousine. I wondered if I should have said yes to this adventure as I sensed Maggie and Laura watching me from the window. However, my mind quickly shifted gears when, with great dignity, the young man in the maroon uniform held open the rear door and waved me in with a black-leather-gloved hand. I stepped into a world completely out of touch with my own. I wasn't used to plush.

"Ensconced in black, suede-like seat cushions, I pretended I was Jackie Kennedy as the smooth, slick machine oozed its way effortlessly up and down familiar hills until it stopped in front of the World Trade Center on the Embarcadero.

"Oh dear, I've done it again haven't I. You've probably never heard of Jackie Kennedy. I'm sorry Luke. Jackie was one of the "queens" of my day.

"Now where was I? Oh yes, on the Embarcadero. The door of that sleek limousine opened as if by magic. I glided out onto the sidewalk and stood in front of one of the most prestigious restaurants in San Francisco.

"As I walked into the foyer, there to greet me was my supervisor, Mr. Metcalf, and his wife. He introduced me to my escort for the evening Mr. John Aikens, President of the Middlin Bank of London. I was also presented to Lord and Lady Montclair—like Mr. Aikens, clients of the bank. Two other members of the higher echelon of the bank and their wives were there also. Why I was chosen for this illustrious occasion will always remain one of the great mysteries of my life.

"The evening turned out to be a truly memorable one.

"During dinner Lord Montclair mentioned he found the game of cribbage quite a relaxing pastime. I had said very little during the evening in an effort to hide my feeling of inadequacy. I also hoped that I might appear aloof and cosmopolitan. But I felt that it was time for me to contribute to the conversation. Casually I agreed that I found cribbage a relaxing pastime also. When everyone had finished the last course, Lord Montclair asked if I would do him the honor of playing a game with him. Trying to maintain my sophisticated air, I answered in the affirmative.

"In a mahogany-paneled room supplied by the management, Lord Montclair and I played two games of cribbage. He legitimately beat me twice.

"Upon returning to the dining room, Mr. Metcalf escorted me into the bar. He asked if I would be willing to show John the seamier side of our fair city. Mr. Metcalf explained that during the evening's conversation, John had mentioned he'd heard a great deal about our 'gold coast' and expressed a desire to take in a few of the night spots. He intimated he'd been quite disappointed on previous trips to have seen only the lofty and refined side of San Francisco.

"I agreed to take him, provided I would not be held responsible if anything untoward happened to him.

"While the others left in limousines, Mr. Metcalf put John and I into a cab. Our first stop was Finoccios. John found it very difficult to believe the gorgeous girls up on the stage were, in fact, members of his own sex. He kept shaking his head, while periodically looking over at me in a perky sort of quizzical way. He continued to shake his head as we left and proceeded down the street toward the Red Garter. There we drank beer, stomped our feet to the rhythm of the banjoes and joined in the fun singing *Bye, Bye Blackbird, Carolina in the Morning, Won't You Come Home Bill Bailey* and *When the Saints Go Marching In.* John had a powerful voice, and everyone ended up standing around our table. I never asked, but I'd be willing to bet dollars to doughnuts John forgot for awhile that he was President of the Middlin Bank of London.

"Next we went to Earthquake McGoons to hear the man who wrote *Won't You Come Home Bill Bailey* play the clarinet. I wish I could remember his name, but it was so long ago. I'd heard him on a number of occasions, but for John's sake I hoped he would sing his famous song of songs. Many times he didn't when he performed at McGoons—only when the spirit moved, and I guess the spirit moved that night. John was exuberant and left feeling as if he'd just witnessed an historic event.

"About 11:30 PM we arrived at Gold Street on Gold Street. So named because the short, dead-end street was 'paved' end to end with gold carpeting. Gold Street attracted patrons by celebrating New Year's Eve *every* night at midnight. As we entered the smoke-filled, crowded nightclub, it became obvious no tables were available. I didn't expect there would be. We pushed our way through the crowd to the bar.

"If I haven't already mentioned it, John was a very short man, probably about five feet four inches. As we stood sipping our drinks, an extremely tall, buxom waitress sauntered by, a tray of drinks precariously balanced on her raised left palm. At least ninety percent of her bosom was exposed and at John's eye level. I gulped. John commented, quite seriously, 'If it wasn't so hot in here, she'd be jolly cold wouldn't she?' I smiled hoping he hadn't noticed my relief.

"The same waitress came back just before midnight to hand out colorful hats and noise makers. She gave the President of the Middlin Bank of London a most provocative wink then jauntily swaggered off to supply other patrons with her doodads of conviviality.

"The clock struck twelve. John and I joined in the celebration and tried to make as much noise as our pint-sized horns would allow. Blushing, he leaned over and pecked me on the cheek. The redness extended to his toes when the bare-bosomed waitress appeared again and kissed him flush on the mouth. At that particular moment, I'm sure, he was indeed a jolly hot English gentleman.

"I've often wondered if, while sipping sherry at his men's club in the heart of London, John ever told the story of the night he celebrated New Year's Eve in San Francisco, on Gold Street in the middle of July.

"The next evening, when I returned from a day at Carmel-by-the-Sea, a large white box sat waiting on my doorstep. It was wrapped in wide, pink satin ribbon tied into a huge pink, satin bow where soft, red roses peeked out from every fold. I was stunned and thought, could it be for me? A tiny, crown-shaped card was trying to hide beneath one of the roses. It read 'Emma.'

"I picked up the box and brought it into the apartment, gingerly placing it on the kitchen table. I just stared at it for awhile. Finally, my hands shaking, I slowly and carefully lifted off the beribboned cover of the lovely but mysterious box. A strong aroma of roses escaped into the air. Nestled in sheets and sheets of pink tissue paper an immense crystal brandy snifter, filled to the brim with tiny pink and white rosebuds, waited for my gasp. I gasped. It was exquisite. On a satiny gold card in the shape of a crown were the hand-written words, 'Thank you for a charming evening. John'

"I felt like a princess."

As Emma relives that regal moment, her words fade into the fire.

Catherine comes in to ask if Emma would like to have lunch by the fire. Emma blinks her eyes and straightens her shoulders.

"Oh, Catherine. Yes, yes, of course, that would be lovely."

Banjoes. In that dream no way I'm playing a banjo.

All is silent except for the sound of flames jumping into the chimney. Emma picks up her knitting just as Catherine returns with her lunch. Catherine nods to Emma and leads Luke into the hallway.

Emma slowly sips the hot, chicken soup. She has saved the saltines to enjoy with her tea. Sometime later, Catherine returns with Luke and stokes the fire before picking up Emma's tray. Swinging her hips and balancing the tray in barmaid fashion, she departs. Emma smiles in appreciation, picks up her knitting again and continues as if there had been no interruption.

"Yes Luke, I had a good time at the bank. But, one night I had dinner and went to a movie with a teller I'd befriended. Her name was Sarah. After the movie, we went into one of the bars nearby for a nightcap. Out of the blue, as we discussed the movie, the bank, the world in general, she asked me to be her lover. Now back at that time a gay lifestyle was pretty much taboo to say the least—even in San Francisco where it was more prevalent than in most parts of the country, except perhaps in Provincetown, Massachusetts. I was totally confounded and frightened. You probably can't understand that at all, but trust me it was that unusual—so much so that I felt I had no other choice but to give Mr. Metcalf my resignation.

"I was very fortunate though because another friend who worked at Kaiser Hospital told me that the Administrator, a Mr. Brandon, had an ad on the bulletin boards for a new secretary. I applied the next day. Mr. Brandon informed me the hospital preferred to hire from within, if possible, but that my application would be kept on file. He called me himself the following week. That man turned out to be the kind of boss I'd only dreamt of.

"I loved working at the hospital. I particularly enjoyed interfacing with the new interns and residents—interns shaking in their boots, residents one step down from God.

"One Friday morning, as my fingers jitterbugged across the typewriter keyboard, I looked up to see one of the new residents smiling down at me. It was a familiar smile. I stared, pointing my finger at him.

"'You're the guy who used to make doughnuts in the window of Brockleman's market on Main Street back in New Hampshire.'

"He laughed, 'Yup, that's me.'

"Life was full of surprises in San Francisco.

"My first Christmas of red geraniums, yellow and white daisies, pink Christmas trees fastened to masts in the Marina, silver and blue Christmas trees glowing in picture windows, no snow, no biting cold and no family turned out to be one of my most joyous. Good friends understood and were determined that it would be.

"It was all so long ago. I remember I almost married a doctor from San Francisco General, but he wanted to spend the rest of his life in the City by the Bay. I thought I loved him, but not quite enough I guess. I couldn't abandon the time-worn traditions of New England. I'd left my heart in New Hampshire. We said goodbye."

Emma pauses. She sees Matt and Monique climbing the ravine. No. I can't go there.

"Anyway, Luke, I began to date a banjo player from the Red Garter, a happy-go-lucky sort of guy named Harry, whose first love was the banjo. We shared the sights and all the night spots; we drove down the peninsula, through the Big Sur, and explored

Hearst Castle, Carmel-by-the-Sea and Monterey. We put up with cricks in our necks to watch the red woods reach for the sky in Muir Woods.

"I particularly remember the evenings we stood on the Golden Gate Bridge and basked in the beauty of a full moon over San Francisco Bay. We watched its gleaming light glitter on the swaying waves—waves content to listen, along with me, to the strains of Harry's banjo filling the air with the lilting notes of *Have You Ever Been Lonely.*

"Am I rambling Luke? Well, bear with me. I'd really like to tell you about the evening Harry and I sat drinking beer and singing our hearts out during one of Harry's breaks at the Red Garter.

"BAM!" The two front doors burst open. We looked up and the notes stuck in our throats. Coming toward us were the San Francisco Forty-Niners. Leo Namolini, a star lineman, sat down at our table. I apologized for staring. He had no neck. His head was just plunked down on his shoulders. He banged on the table and shouted for ten pitchers of beer. It wasn't long before the rest of the team joined us. We all laughed and sang and sang, but after downing the ten pitchers and a few more, they disappeared into the night.

"You know, Luke, if one doesn't join the human race, nothing unusual is ever going to happen.

"I don't think Mr. Brandon ever really believed I had spent an evening drinking and singing with his precious and prized Forty Niners.

"Do you know if the Forty Niners still play football for San Francisco?"

Catherine taps on the door and tiptoes toward the hearth where she adds wood to the fading fire.

She was like really cool for way back then. Muffin would never have left home or gone into a bar. Muffin? Muffin? Who's Muffin? Who're the Forty Niners?

Catherine turns away from the fire and tells Emma dinner will be served in about an hour.

Emma smiles and nods, "Thank you Catherine."

She gets up and limps toward the door as Catherine helps Luke out of his chair.

In the hallway she smiles at Catherine and says to Luke, "See you in the morning, young man."

That morning Emma lies in bed for a long time. Her whole life runs through her head. Matt and Monique smile at her from some unknown, faraway place. But no, she won't go there yet, not yet. Soon… .

Her will pulls Emma to her feet and she prepares for the coming day. On her way out the door she goes back for her yellow sweater. She's determined to make this day a bright and shiny one.

As Emma finishes her second cup of coffee, Catherine leans over her shoulder and tells her the fire is lit. "Luke seems to be waiting for you." she whispers.

Emma takes the elevator to the second floor and enters the little sewing room. She looks at Luke and feels Catherine might be right. She sits down and begins to rock.

"Good morning Luke. I'm a little late. I just felt like another cup of coffee.

"Let's see, where did I leave off? Oh yes, that evening with the Forty Niners. Well, it was shortly after that I found myself scurrying around the apartment on a Saturday afternoon attempting to pack for a trip to Napa Valley. I had planned to join Laura and Maggie there. They had left the night before. As I crossed the living room for the umteenth time, I stopped and said to myself, 'Whoa! What are you doing?' My knees collapsed and I slid to the floor, not wanting to go anywhere. I felt like whoever it was that said, 'Stop world. I want to get off.'

"I dialed the motel in Napa Valley and left a message with the desk clerk for the girls in 9B. It read, 'Not coming. No emergency. Not to worry, I'm just not coming.'

"I got up, grabbed a can of beer out of the refrigerator and sat at a table in the picture window. Laura and I so often sat there to watch the world go by—more specifically, the entire phenomenon that was San Francisco.

"I inhaled the relief of just sitting with nothing to do, nowhere to go, the apartment all to myself. I had found a buried treasure—diamonds of time and gold of quiet solitude.

"My mind wandered into the past and strayed toward my future. I didn't notice the sun slip behind a darkening horizon until tiny white lights twinkling in the distance seemed to be falling haphazardly from the sky. I watched them for a long, long time. Then a thought disturbed my reverie.

"The view never changed—beautiful but always the same except when it disappeared into the fog rolling in from the Bay. The same red geraniums across the street, the same white and yellow daisies peeking out behind rocks up on the Peaks, the same calla lilies, palm trees and wind—no matter what time of year.

"I asked myself what month it was. I knew I wouldn't find the answer looking out at California's landscape. It's not like New Hampshire's where leaves on swaying maple trees turn brilliant shades of red and gold in October and where from November through February snow defies the wind and piles higher and higher upon limbs of elm, oak and pine. Where in March the lingering snow disappears and leaves bare branches cold and lonesome until May rolls around to clothe the shivering arms in soft, green leaves.

"I missed the changing seasons. No, I longed for them. I guess I'd never understood my need in just that way before.

"Thoughts of permanently returning to New England sent my mind in search of the people and places I assumed were locked away there from trips I'd taken back to New England during the past four years. Why weren't the Rocky Mountains clearer? For that matter, what happened to Pikes Peak, the Sierra Nevada Mountains and the Grand Canyon? My memories seem to have faded, and I didn't have any pictures—I didn't even own a camera. I'd always preferred mental pictures. It never occurred to me that memories dim as time flies by.

"I went in search of paper and pencil to note the things that were important to me, what I enjoyed. I wrote down solitude and ambling time. I listed variety as necessary. I added I probably should think about getting a camera.

"The lights continued to sprinkle their sparkle in competition with the shimmering moon. As I watched, it occurred to me there were many more places in the world I hadn't seen—Europe, the Islands, Russia, Australia, Asia. *Whoa* again. I could never see them all, let alone remember them all. I could never be an integral part of any one of them…just an outsider looking in. I didn't like being an outsider looking in.

"I added that to my list.

"The words on the paper floated up into my brain and rattled around and around. When they settled in place, I got up and went into the bedroom. From the bottom drawer of the bureau I pulled out a three-ring binder and flipped through it. I found the poem I was looking for and read the last few lines.

Till 'cross its lace-edged waves
I hear a breath upon the air
Like me, just be,
What matter where?

"How wise the sea, Luke. W*here* doesn't matter, does it? I looked out the window, then up at the lovely opaline moon. It seemed to say, 'I'll see you in New Hampshire where you'll be content just *being* Emma.'

"From the same bottom drawer I retrieved my box of treasures. In it I found the Christmas card from Uncle Harry. Do you remember Uncle Harry? He was the Santa Claus I watched for through my grandmother's cold, glass windowpane—the Santa who frightened me. His card that year had a note inside. I've always remembered the last two lines, 'We hope you will be with us all next year. I think you have seen the other part of this country of ours, now come home and see and enjoy the best.' It's so comforting, Luke, to have these things to remember.

"Laura and Maggie returned from Napa Valley on Sunday evening. I told them I was going home. They tried to talk me out of it; we cried, but they eventually understood. It was difficult for them though. They'd never had a problem allowing their inner selves to just be. Wherever they were, they were. They couldn't fathom that I had been searching for myself. But once they did, they found it hard to understand why I couldn't be me in San Francisco. I explained, while I loved them both and the City too, California was not where I wanted my newfound self to bloom and grow. New England, with its changing seasons and comfortable traditions, was, for me, the only place to live the *now* and look forward to what might be.

"Two weeks later on a cold, windy morning, I hugged Maggie and Laura goodbye then stepped into my new red Falcon. It was packed so tightly there was barely enough room for my purse, let alone me.

"When I looked up for a last goodbye, my friends were disappearing into a thick, roiling fog that had surreptitiously rolled in from the Bay. Desperately, I wanted another hug, but the wind refused to allow an open door. Before rolling up the window, tears running down my cheeks, I groped and found an outstretched hand. How tightly I squeezed it…then left in it a long white envelope before I quickly sped off down Alvarado—a slight aroma of Chanel No. 5 lingering in my nostrils.

"I knew Maggie and Laura would stand in the fog till the air was silent. I imagined them climbing the invisible stairs and going into our apartment, where they would open my envelope."

From the pocket of her sweater Emma retrieves her copy of its contents and reads:

"Laura and Maggie,

You're used to struggling with the many words I love to shift and tumble. Here's another bunch…

Moon, oh lovely moon,
Your misty rays
Drift softly through air
Crisp as the fallen snow
And gently brush
A sleeping wreath
Hung low on the old shed door.
A crimson ribbon wakes and

Winks at its friend in the sky,
Who reveals as well
The sultry soil where
Drooping fronds and milky fruit
Hang high in swaying trees,
Their roots at rest
In the cooling sand.

Mystical, auric sphere
Afloat in earth's celestial lid,
Keep vigil
O'er this fickle world below,
Hold constant your visage to
Those who lift their eyes in wonder
But care not
What prods that silvery face
To spread its light
O'er earth's darkened ways,
Comforting each wandering soul,
Bringing softness into the night
Where young lovers woo.

Inspired, the moment
I sensed, I knew
Your smiling glow,
'Mid shining stars,
Obscures your ancient wisdom
Calling out through
Time and stardust.
Though never heard,
Never heeded
Throughout these many years,
It bellows now
Within my deafened ears,
'Use the gifts been given thee
To be whom you shall ever be.'

Love Good Friends—I'll be in touch. *Emma*"

Emma rocks in the silence, then says, "I know Luke, you don't think you have anything to go back to.

"But it doesn't always have to be that way, not if you begin now to fashion a new life…if you decide it's worth facing what the world has to offer. If you do, without even realizing it, you'll create a past—a past to fall back on, if and when you ever need it. I think you'll be glad you did when the world seems to turn the color of fading autumn leaves and slips through your fingers into those of the inconstant young.

"You and I are many, many years apart in age and experience. My life is at an end…yours is just beginning. As much as I'd love to, I can't give you, or even lend you, my years and years of living.

"Oh, I know my stories have no relevance to what your life was or can be. I lived a long time ago in a different world—sometimes I think on a different planet. All I've hoped and prayed for is that my stories would somehow awaken in you the reality that one's life must be lived—lived in a world of numerous opportunities to enjoy its wonders, explore its possibilities or grasp its chances for love and affection. The choice is yours—fame and fortune or obscurity. Oh my dear Luke, you can toss your life away, follow the crowd or listen to your heart and be whom you shall ever be.

"What a life is or may be depends solely on the aspirations of the individual to whom it belongs. I tried very hard to allow my life its opportunities. I pray you'll do the same for yours."

It wasn't my imagination. They're back. I can hear them. I don't want to lose even one.

Rhythm, melody and harmony have always been an integral part of Luke's life…his spirituality as well as his humanity. Of course his life has been empty, black and cavernous all these past many months without notes dominating the air. But now they dance around him like prancing, laughing clowns waiting for the parade to begin. They have never seemed so clear, so dear.

As Emma rocks and stares into the fire, an ethereal feeling creeps over her and she turns her head toward Luke. His chair is rocking in unison with hers. Emma's heart doesn't know whether to stop or leap out of her chest. She struggles with changing emotions, afraid to move. She does not want to make a mistake. Once again she gazes into the fire, then stands up and walks over to Luke. She commands her arthritic knees to bend and kneels before him. Her tears, glistening in the firelight, flow freely as she lays her head upon his knees. His hand lightly strokes her soft white hair and he whispers, "I bought a dream."

Catherine opens the door to their sanctuary and catches her breath. She watches for a few moments and quietly closes the door, standing stunned in the hallway.

"Sure and I wonder what he said to her."

She lingers for a moment then reaches for the doorknob…but her arm falls slowly to her side.

"No, I mustn't. Sure and these precious moments belong only to Emma and Luke."

Although she has never really believed in God, Catherine, deep in thought, walks toward the chapel where she kneels and stares into an atmosphere replete with the odor of incense long since extinguished. She perceives a kind of spirituality emanating from dust-filled light cascading through stained-glass windows.

Slowly, she absorbs her soul as it radiates from a woman kneeling before a hand-hewn tomb, from an angel with wings spread wide, from a man hung high upon unfinished wood and from a little child kept warm by the breath of a mule.

She looks up when an aged hand squeezes her arm. Emma and Catherine pray silently together, their heads bent low.

Time stands still for these two women—Emma's heart overflowing with thanks, Catherine awed at having encountered her soul.

Emma sighs realizing that she, like time, must continue to move forward, though relieved not for much longer. With great effort, she lifts herself to a standing position and walks slowly toward the door. Catherine follows and watches until she disappears into her room. Needing just a little more time, Catherine leans against the wall for a minute or two before going down the hall to the small sewing room where she finds Luke rocking silently by a disappearing fire. She walks over to his chair to help him up, but he pulls away. A moment later, he gets up.

"Which way?"

"Straight ahead."

When he reaches the door, Catherine, smiling from ear to ear, says, "Take a left and the elevator is the third door on your right. When you get to it, the button to the right opens the doors. When you're inside, as you face the closed doors, the button you want is the third one up on the right. When you step out of the elevator turn right. Your room is the second one on the left." Luke bows his head and says, "Thank you."

Upon entering her room, Emma immediately sits down at the old computer that Catherine so thoughtfully had had brought in for her a few weeks ago from the small sewing room where it had been tucked away for years. She smiles remembering how relieved they were when Catherine plugged it in and it worked; *Word* was still there and the printer still able to do its job. Quickly she fills in the unfinished fourth paragraph of a letter she has spent many, many hours composing. Her missive now at last ready, Emma prints it out and places it in an envelope.

Catherine smothers the smoldering embers and gathers up Emma's knitting before going down the hall to Emma's room. She needs to talk about Luke. Emma greets her with a warm smile and invites her to sit down. Catherine drops the knitting on the bed and pulls a small Victorian rocker up next to Emma and gently takes her hands before quietly saying, "Luke won't be led any more. Sure and he got up by himself and asked for directions." Emma frees her hands and places them on Catherine's rosy cheeks and smiles, "I'm not surprised, Catherine. He's an independent young man and he'll need that self-reliance as he makes his way in this world."

"He also said thank you. Imagine. Sure and you did it, Emma, you really did, but I have to admit, I thought you were crazy when you started all this, 'cause, frankly, I was convinced the lad was a lost soul."

Emma's smile seems tired as she admits she thought she was a bit crazy herself. The two women reminisce a few more minutes before Emma interrupts Catherine to ask her to get an envelope addressed to Luke in the top, right-hand drawer of her desk. When Catherine returns with the envelope, Emma holds it in her hand for just a lingering moment. Her last story had taken a long time to type. How thankful she'd been for the old word processor. With a sigh she gives up the envelope to Catherine.

"Put this in your pocket and give it to Luke at the appropriate time."

"But Emma, how..."

"Shh now, no questions; you'll know what to do."

"Catherine, I don't think I'll be down to dinner. I'm very tired. It's been quite a day, and I'm not a bit hungry. I'd like to retire early."

Catherine has a few more questions teetering on the edge of her tongue, but somehow knows she mustn't ask them. She looks at Emma sitting in her chair by the window.

She's forgotten I'm here.

A twinge of foreboding creeps over her as she moves slowly toward the door. Before leaving, she turns and murmurs, "Ring if you need me."

Meanwhile, Luke finds his room and opens the door. He lies down on the bed and puts his hands behind his head.

I'm Luke. I have a friend—a real friend. And I have my music, music I won't ever, ever hide again. I'll be me, only me.

I've got a family too.

He hears his long-lost notes yelling, "How much longer must we be silent?"

Oh, not long. I can't believe my luck; you waited for me. Be patient just a little longer and, once more, my guitar will be your passage to the world of sound. I'm going to gather you into unbelievable music that will immortalize Emma's stories. You'll become a lilting melody for the box wrapped in wide, pink ribbon; a country tune for the saga of her landlady; melodramatic notes for her love of the stage and ragtime for San Francisco. But especially because she brought you back, haunting harmony for a song beginning, My blood flows warm.

I'll ask Muffin to bring my guitar, and I'll play it for Emma. I'll play whatever she wants to hear for as long as she wants to listen.

The next morning, Emma's place at the breakfast table is empty. Catherine hurries upstairs to Emma's room. She stands in front of the door until she finds the courage to open it. Taking a deep breath, she turns the doorknob and watches as the door inches slowly into the room. She hesitates, then enters. Emma—lifeless, her head bowed—is where Catherine had left her the night before. Catherine tiptoes slowly over to her friend and kneels by her chair. The world seems empty somehow and a lot less friendly. She looks out at Emma's mighty mountain and sees a young Emma, her long skirt billowing in the wind, her hair blowing in undulating waves as she stands on its peak shading her eyes and looking toward the heavens. Then she is gone and with her that period of time when humanity loved, cared, and watched out for one another. Catherine wonders if the world will ever again know a time such as Emma's.

She gets up and places her cheek on Emma's soft, white hair. Reluctantly, she moves away and walks slowly toward the door. Her hand on the doorknob hesitates. She turns and whispers, "Thank you for bein' around so long, for bein' part of my life. Sure and if you hadn't, I'd never have known there was more to me than flesh 'n blood. I'd never have known how the world used to be. Sure and weren't you lucky? Oh, and Emma, I understand now my son's need to place his talent behind his heart."

She stops in the chapel for a few moments before going downstairs to inform the powers-that-be Emma has passed away and to make the cremation arrangements Emma had requested.

When she's done what she has to do, Catherine calls Margaret and relates what she'd seen in the small sitting room the day before. She then adds, "Sure and Emma's job's done Margaret; she's gone home." Margaret hears her tears and remains silent for a few moments.

"I am truly sorry, Catherine. I know how close you two were. It is very difficult to lose a friend. She was Luke's friend too. Have you told him?"

"Sure and I haven't told him yet; perhaps you'd like to. I assume you'll be comin'."

Margaret assures her she'll leave immediately. Catherine hangs up the phone and slowly climbs the stairs to Luke's room—the elevator will get her there too quickly. She finds him sitting by the window. Relieved he cannot see her tears, she gives him directions to the small sewing room, where she has lit what she hopes will be a comforting fire. She leaves then to take care of all those others who need her too.

It seems like no time at all when Margaret comes through the front door and hurries over to Catherine. With a hug she asks, "What happened?"

"Sure and our Emma passed away last night sittin' in her chair lookin' out at the stars."

Margaret reflects for a moment then inquires about the funeral arrangements. Catherine tells her, "Emma's body is now in the hands of Mr. Carter, the funeral director. Sure and Emma had specifically requested there be no fuss and that cremation was her primary choice. Her exact words were, 'Catherine, when all the apples have been eaten, there's no further need for their container. When my spirit has returned home, cremate the body that held it for just a little while."

Margaret doesn't hold back her tears and puts an arm around Catherine's shoulders. As they walk toward the elevator she asks if Luke is up in the little sewing room. Catherine nods.

Before Margaret enters the elevator, Catherine adds, "Sure and I'll be makin' the arrangements for a memorial service at Our Lady of the Mountain Catholic Church in North Conway. I don't think Emma would be considerin' that too much fuss, do you?" Margaret shakes her head and answers, "Let me know when."

As Margaret leaves the elevator, she hesitates just a moment before hurrying down the hallway to the familiar door. Taking a deep breath, she opens it and watches as her son quietly rocks by a fire prancing to nowhere. Her familiar perfume permeates the air. Slowly, she walks toward Luke and gently kisses him on the forehead before sitting down in Emma's chair.

A quiet but strong voice asks, "Where's Emma?"

They are the first words she's heard her son say in over two years.

"Her job is done, Luke. She has gone home."

Margaret sits quietly watching her son rock back and forth, back and forth. She longs to hear him speak again, but only silent tears lay bare his feelings.

She'll always be my friend.

"You were so fortunate, Luke, to have had your time with Emma. Think of all you learned about that grand old world she lived in long before you or I were even born.

"Emma was not the only one trying to hold onto that wonderful world was she Luke? I understand now; I have not ever let go either. But perhaps now you can better understand why I held on so tightly. I realize I have never even tried to be part of the only world you have ever known. Forgive me. Emma made me see how much I have tried to tuck you into my safe existence.

"She understood the necessity for progress far better than I. What she did not understand was why going forward meant leaving human dignity and kindness behind. Secretly, I think she sort of hoped you would help the world journey back into the one she loved so much…back into a time when men cared and men shared.

"I am thankful for the short time I spent with her, particularly one afternoon not long ago when we stood by the railing watching the mountains rise high in front of the sky while the little town of Jackson lay quietly at their feet. In a far-away voice she whispered, 'America—ours to love, ours to serve.' I remarked what a lovely thought it was. She told me the words belonged to a man named Telier who had enriched the lives of those who were lucky enough to discover his enchanting, bucolic paintings."

Margaret pauses before continuing.

"I told Emma about your music, Luke. I did not think you would mind if I shared my pride with her. She prayed every day that you had not lost your talent and that some day you too would enrich the lives of many.

"One day I heard her ask the mountains, 'Why can't a young man from Massachusetts reverse a trend that started six decades ago?' She explained that a group of teenagers from England, way back in the fifties, had completely changed the way music was composed, instrumentalized and sung. Then she insisted that you could be just as influential. You know how she loved a challenge. She hoped her young man from Massachusetts would reintroduce the world to melody, harmony and lyrics written to inspire not to satisfy appetites. Oh, I understand, dear, one person's trash is another's treasure...but it *was* Emma's dream.

"She loved you sweetheart, but not as much as I do. Will you help me to escape my fear for you? May I share your world? Will you let me listen to your music?"

Mother and son rock in unison before the fire.

Muffin is more than just manners and appearances. She loves me.

After softly tapping on the door, Catherine enters and goes directly over to Luke. She puts her arm around his shoulders and looks inquiringly at Margaret, who stares into the flames still prancing to nowhere.

Catherine's presence does not intrude on Margaret and Luke, who are in a zone they have never shared before.

Catherine smiles for she knows now that Emma wanted her to give the envelope to Margaret. She places it in Margaret's lap and kisses Luke softly on the forehead. Neither of them is aware of Catherine gently closing the door.

Margaret looks down at the envelope. She picks it up and gives it a hopeful squeeze. Not knowing exactly what to expect, she rises and walks over to Luke. Awakened by the movement, her perfume drifts slowly through the air. He reaches out for her. Margaret's arms go around her son pulling him close to her pounding heart—the envelope still clutched in her hand. Luke slumps against his mother, and she squeezes him closer. After some moments, she reluctantly releases him and murmurs, "Catherine just handed me an envelope. It says in large capital letters A Bunch of Words for Luke. Would you like me to read them?" Luke nods his head. Margaret returns to her rocker and begins to read.

"November 2, 2025

Dear Luke,

My silent friend, I haven't left you behind. How could I? My heart sings it is so happy for you. And I shall never, ever silence its song.

Think about the air for a minute. You can't see it can you? Yet you know it's there.

I also ask you to think about that elusive something we call destiny. I know it took me a long time before I realized I had an inescapable fate that would, some day, place me before God wrapped in my cloak of deeds.

If I'd been aware of it sooner, I wouldn't have wasted so much time. I'd have started earlier to try to make the world around me a happier place, a more peaceful place, an easier place.

Decide what you want to do with your life, Luke, then do it.

With confidence I can tell you that as long as you're able to lay your head upon the pillow and fall fast asleep, you will live a happy and satisfying life.

With that bit of "whatever" off my chest, I shall finish where I left off when your chair began to rock and you let me know you were back and had a dream.

Dreams, you know, are heralds of destiny.

And now settle back and listen to the demise of my frivolity.

I traveled the southern route of this beautiful country on my way home and never once did I feel lonesome. I'll let you in on a little secret. I've always considered myself pretty good company.

Me, myself and I paid $25 a very large amount in 1962 for a pair of cheap, poorly fitting, plastic sunglasses. Well, what can one do when one is in the middle of the Mojave Desert, squinting painfully at the sun, and only a one-pump gas station and store as far as the eye can see? The glasses proved a wise investment as I traveled across the desert, through Arizona, New Mexico and into the Texas Panhandle.

My trip, on the whole, produced little along the lines of adventure, but I did experience one or two amusing incidents.

One occurred as I drove along a Texas highway late on a hot and sultry afternoon. In spite of the hour, a blazing sun poured its molten lava down on me and the uncountable steer roaming across interminable plains on both sides of the road. While I watched, they slowly disappeared off the edge of the world.

My mouth watered for a thick, juicy, rare, sizzling steak. Knowing I'd probably never have another opportunity to taste fresh, genuine Texas beef, I began to look for a restaurant. A few miles later, I drove into the parking lot of what could have been a saloon on the set of a western movie. As I hopped out of the car, I remember wondering where all the cars in the parking lot had come from. I hadn't seen a town or a house in miles.

I pushed open the swinging doors and made my way through a howling crowd to an empty booth on the far side of the combination bar and dining room. I sat down and tried not to look too awed by all the hootin' and hollerin'. I fully expected to see Billy the Kid come bursting through the door with his six-guns blazing. But of course he didn't.

Oh dear Luke, I do keep forgetting how young you are. You've undoubtedly never heard of Billy the Kid. Ask your mother to find out if there's a talking book out about him. If there is, listen to it. He was quite a guy.

I was amused as I watched a hip-swinging cowgirl dos-a-dos her way toward me. She was obviously enjoying the rhythm of the twanging guitars and stomping feet. When she reached me, she handed me a menu and asked what I'd like to drink. I told her ice water and a rare steak with all the fixings. She nodded and shuffled off, then turned and asked where I was from. I smiled and said, "New Hampshire." From her reaction I have to guess she heard New Hampshah since she replied, "I've never met anyone from New Hampshire. You sure sound funny."

She must have pointed me out to her fellow Texans. Why else did all those six-gallon hats turn in my direction?

The thought of that sizzling, thick, rare piece of beef can still, to this day, excite my palate. I shall forever consider it one of the truly extraordinary, culinary experiences of my life. When I attempted to pay for it, the cowgirl with the swinging hips winked and informed me a gentleman had already done so. Flabbergasted I asked, as I scanned the restaurant, 'Which one?' She shrugged her shoulders and said, 'He's already left.' I put my wallet back in my purse and left too, feeling a bit apprehensive as I went out into the parking lot. But I needn't have.

The next day, traveling through Oklahoma, I thought I was going to die of the heat. The humidity had to have been at least ninety-five percent. I spotted a lone tree the only one for miles—coming up on my left and pulled in underneath it. All I wanted to do was rest in its shade with an ice-cold coke. I took one from the cooler on the front seat and sat on the ground, thinking about the hundreds and hundreds of miles that still lie ahead.

I looked up as a huge eighteen-wheeler pulled in beside me. The driver jumped down and asked if I'd like some help changing my flat tire. I looked up at him as if he had seven heads and assured him I did not have a flat tire; I'd just stopped to rest and cool off. He insisted I had a flat tire. He was right. I couldn't believe it, and, of course, welcomed his assistance. When I opened the trunk, his jaw dropped. I promised him there was a tire underneath there somewhere. Without further ado, we both began to unload the trunk and finally found the spare tire. Sporting invisible wings, my guardian angel cheerfully changed the tire. I tried to pay him, but he would have none of that. He even helped me repack the trunk before he drove off whistling *It's A Long Way to Tipperary.*

As I drove along those hundreds and hundreds of miles through Arkansas, Tennessee, Virginia and Pennsylvania, I couldn't help but wonder what the silent architecture and multi-colored fauna and flora thought of my bright red Falcon as it went racing past. I waved at more than a few. I also returned the friendly greetings of hundreds of swaying leaves.

When a sign by the side of the road read Pennsylvania, my heart began to pound. The scenery was beginning to look and feel like New England. In Connecticut, I couldn't sing loud enough. Now there's the advantage of traveling alone—I've never been able to carry a tune.

Then, one afternoon about three o'clock—how I remember the time I don't know—New Hampshire welcomed me with the open arms of pine, oak and maple. I was home.

My favorite part of the world burst forth with striking color, as I knew it would. Fall bloomed not by chance. I had planned it that way.

After spending a few weeks with Hannah and Chocolate, I found a job and an apartment in quaint, historic Boston. I assure you, it was quaint way back then. History and old things always having fascinated me, where else would I go but to a city abounding in silent antiquities? Luckily, Boston's bustling streets and hurtling subways welcomed the stranger in their midst.

I accepted a secretarial position with three aspiring attorneys but found I really preferred a medical atmosphere. So the employment section of the Boston Globe became required reading. One Sunday morning I spotted an ad for an Administrative Assistant to the Administrator of a prestigious Boston Clinic. I applied Monday morning and was given an interview with the Personnel Manager. Toward the end of my interview, he escorted me into the outer office and asked if I'd wait while he telephoned Mr. Brandon in San Francisco. Do you remember my telling you about Mr. Brandon, Luke? Well, I never learned what he had to say, but whatever it was it clinched the position for me.

I found an apartment overlooking the Charles River, and you can imagine my surprise and delight when I found out my friend Peg—you remember, the one from Hartford—had also come to Boston and lived in the same building.

We both took advantage of the Harvard Extension courses, and I joined a theatre group in Belmont, a Boston suburb.

Many weekends I spent in New Hampshire with Hannah and Chocolate.

One particular Sunday afternoon changed the course of my life. It was a stormy day. The snow blew and the wind howled.

Hannah had promised her parish priest she would collect donations and pledges for the Catholic Charities drive that afternoon. She asked if I'd like to come along, and I was more than happy to do so. We spent all afternoon canvassing the neighborhood. How we laughed at the snow, jumping and spitting. Snow gets very angry you know when it can't have its own way.

As we made the first ruts through mounds of the nettled flakes mounting higher and higher on each street we traveled, Hannah did her best to convince me I should stay the night and return to Boston in the morning. She knew very well that, without fail, I went back to Boston late on Sunday afternoon. I hated the early morning congestion on Routes 3 and 128. With all the snow, I knew only too well that traffic the next morning would be torturous. My preference definitely leaned toward battling snow in the dark to sitting impatient, sputtering at the immovable congestion.

We finished our canvas and went home to enjoy a cup of Earl Grey tea. While we were patting ourselves on the back for a job well done, the telephone rang. Hannah answered and, with a quizzical glint in her eye, handed the phone to me. A fellow named Matt Duprey was on the other end of the line. I knew him from my high school days. He'd been a very popular athlete.

Matt asked if I'd be free the following weekend to join him at a dinner party being planned by his investment club to celebrate its tenth anniversary. I accepted.

The following morning found me sitting in the torturous, immovable traffic.

All week I wondered if Matt had changed, gotten fat maybe. After all, twenty years had gone by since I'd seen him. I remembered his being quite handsome and couldn't figure out why he was still single.

The following Saturday evening found him still quite handsome—not fat at all, just bald. He was quite shy, but in spite of that, I found him an extremely easy person to be with. I hadn't remembered his being shy, but then I'd never known him very well.

When we'd dated about six months, he invited me to spend a weekend up in the White Mountains. We stayed at The New England Inn here in Jackson and explored many of the mountain trails in this area.

On Saturday night in the Inn's dining room, we were discussing the Bruins, Boston's hockey team, when Matt mentioned it had always been his dream to watch the Canadiens play at the Forum in Montreal. We had spent many an evening watching the Bruins play at the Boston Garden—you'd know it as the Fleet Center. Not my favorite thing to do, but, oh my, how Matt loved hockey. Anyway, out of the blue, he announced he thought Montreal would be a terrific spot for a honeymoon. Not sure where that came from, I softly and hesitantly agreed. I didn't mention I'd often dreamed of a honeymoon in the Bahamas.

Later that evening, sitting in front of the Inn's large fireplace sipping Mateus Rose´, Matt asked if I'd consider marrying him. Silly, I know, but the first thing that came into my mind was the number of times I had heard friends' husbands say to them, "You know, I never really asked you to marry me." And I remembered thinking, "No man will ever say that to me."

So I said to Matt, "You'll never know unless you ask." He did, and we were married a few months later. We spent our honeymoon at the Forum in Montreal. I loved being there because he was there. He reminded me of a little boy with a new puppy. Oh, to be sure, he thought I loved hockey too. He never knew about my Bahamas dream.

A year later our little daughter Monique arrived and shared our love and our lives. Twenty years later, I lost them both to an avalanche in Tuckerman Ravine—a skier's haven tucked into the eastern side of our towering Mount Washington.

I saw it happen, Luke.

I watched from the porch of Tuckerman Shelter as they climbed up into the bowl of the ravine. With me was a young man, about your age, who had been blinded after losing control of his skis some years before. We were both absorbing the excitement and beauty of Tuckerman Ravine in the springtime.

Without warning a huge block of ice broke from the top of the headwall. Ice and snow hurtled down on Matt and Monique. Before my eyes they disappeared. The young man helped me through the hours that followed. I don't know what would have happened to me if he hadn't been there. We kept in touch until he died about twenty years ago.

After the funerals, the world was a very lonely place. Chocolate had died before I married Matt, and Hannah died when Monique was thirteen years old. My dear friend Anne of course had to return to her family in California. Unfortunately, I had never taken the time to make other close friends, so there was no one to turn to except myself. But I didn't realize I was there for me for some time. You see, I thought my life had also ended in Tuckerman Ravine.

I'm not going to burden you any further, dear Luke, with more details of my life except to tell you that eventually I found myself again. I sold my Victorian home and moved into a pleasant, three-room apartment. I found a secretarial job in a lawyer's office that was only temporary while I studied, sometimes all night, preparing to take the real estate exam. Not having studied for some time, I found it very tedious and difficult to concentrate. I was ready though when time came to take the exam. Somehow I managed to pass it. I made a comfortable life for myself and spent my time writing poetry and enjoying the camaraderie and sociability of the other agents.

As the years went by I discovered I truly loved houses—particularly the really old ones. Evcntually I ended up not selling but restoring them.

As I kept myself busy with these restorative challenges, I took advantage of every opportunity to string together my provocative words. I labored contentedly to be successful at both endeavors. And I discovered they had a great deal in common. Each involved stimulating and satisfying the senses. Each required the creation of harmony and balance in order to progress smoothly from one thought to another or from one room to another.

So, there you are, Luke…my life.

My plea is that you allow *your* life its adventures.

I am more than well aware of how difficult it is to live with loss. But live with it we must. The pain never ends, but it does diminish when we put aside self-preoccupation, when we make sure we never waste the present and when we take time to whistle *It's A Long Way to Tipperary*, pay for a sizzling steak, write a poem or sprinkle notes upon a staff.

The houses kept me busy, yes, but it was primarily the words that persistently called out for my attention. They drifted aimlessly till I helped them lessen the sorrow of a friend, lighten the burden of another or share their joy. Each word's dependence turned out to be my salvation. Your notes drift too, for they're helpless without you. No one will ever gather them together quite the way you do.

I have gathered a few last words, shifting and tumbling them into my final message.

Watch the distant stars
Silently dim and fade away.
See the sun rise slowly
To filter its beams
Through ashen clouds,

Nudging the floating
Grays toward
Salmon hues
No painter has
Upon his palette.

Savor the awe
Of its splendor
Shimmering
Off a farmhouse
Asleep and unaware
It sparkles like a diamond
In its quiet, emerald field,
As a day begins
Never to begin again.

Once more
Hear the call
To journey forth,
With freedom's choice,
Down separate roads
Of goals and dreams
Which matter nought
They guide toward fame
Or a life obscure,
'Tis the soul survives,
To last, to endure.

You know Luke, it never occurred to me until right this minute. Some day, I might be remembered as a lyricist.

I'll be with you always, *Emma*"

Margaret folds the paper and puts it back in the envelope before removing several other pieces of paper, which she places in her son's hand.

"Emma wanted you to have her poetry."

Luke presses the sheets of paper to his heart and rocks and rocks, then stops.

"She *will* be remembered as a lyricist."

Sitting forward in his chair, he stares toward the fire seeming to inhale its comfort…or is it Emma's presence he feels?

Margaret sits still, waiting. When the fire's warmth vanishes into the embers, Luke whispers, "Muffin, I want to say goodbye and then I'd like to go home."

Margaret reaches over and squeezes his free hand. Her love envelops him as she gets up from the rocker and places her arm around his shoulders.

"There is no need to say goodbye, dear. Emma will never be very far away.

"Yeah, I know Muffin. I wouldn't leave without her. I want to say goodbye to Catherine. She's pretty cool too."

"All right, dear. When you have said goodbye, we will pack your things and be on our way. But we will come back for Emma's memorial service. Perhaps you would like to play some of your music for her."

"Oh yeah, I would…I will."

"I will go now and find Catherine so you can let her know what you would like to play for Emma."

Catherine is in the tiny chapel. Margaret kneels down beside her and whispers, "Luke wants to see you before we leave. He is up in the little sewing room."

The two women walk out of the chapel and down the hallway glowing in the warmth of an inner peace—the gift of Emma's final deed.